The Haunting of Horse Island

"I hear something," Bess said. "It sounds like thunder. But it can't be—there isn't a cloud in the sky."

"I hear it, too," said George. The thundering sound was growing louder by the moment.

"It's coming from that direction," Nancy said, pointing to a stretch of clear land that, like a hallway, separated the woods into two sections. The sound kept growing louder and louder until it became an almost deafening rumble.

"Oh, no!" gasped Bess. An amazing sight had suddenly appeared from around a bend in the clearing.

"Horses!" yelled George above the noise.

"Get out of the way!" Nancy screamed at her friends.

Galloping at them was a herd of wild, stampeding horses!

Nancy Drew
Mystery Stories

Available from MINSTREL Books

98

NANCY DREW®

THE HAUNTING OF HORSE ISLAND

CAROLYN KEENE

A MINSTREL® BOOK

PUBLISHED BY POCKET BOOKS

New York   London   Toronto   Sydney   Tokyo   Singapore

This book is a work of fiction. Names, characters, places and incidents are either the product of the author's imagination or are used fictitiously. Any resemblance to actual events or locales or persons, living or dead, is entirely coincidental.

A MINSTREL PAPERBACK *ORIGINAL*

 A Minstrel Book published by
POCKET BOOKS, a division of Simon & Schuster Inc.
1230 Avenue of the Americas, New York, NY 10020

Copyright © 1990 by Simon & Schuster Inc.
Cover art copyright © 1990 Aleta Jenks
Produced by Mega-Books of New York, Inc.

All rights reserved, including the right to reproduce
this book or portions thereof in any form whatsoever.
For information address Pocket Books, 1230 Avenue
of the Americas, New York, NY 10020

ISBN: 0-671-69284-4

First Minstrel Books printing December 1990

10 9 8 7 6 5 4 3

NANCY DREW, NANCY DREW MYSTERY STORIES,
A MINSTREL BOOK and colophon are registered trademarks
of Simon & Schuster Inc.

Printed in the U.S.A.

Contents

THE HAUNTING
OF HORSE ISLAND

1

A Mountain Retreat

"Just think!" said Bess Marvin from the back seat of the car Nancy Drew was driving. "A whole week at Triple Tree Lake. Swimming, sunning, eating—and no scary mysteries to solve!"

Nancy eased the car the girls had rented around a curve in the road and winked at Bess's cousin George Fayne, who was in the passenger seat next to her. "That's right," Nancy said. "Unless, of course, the ghosts decide to cause trouble!"

"What?" Bess cried, her blue eyes wide. She leaned forward and hung her elbows over the front seat. "Nobody ever told me there were ghosts at the Steadman Resort! George, is that why they asked us to come—so Nancy could solve their ghost mystery?" She hooked some loose strands of straw blond hair behind her ear and looked worriedly at her cousin.

George turned and grinned at Bess. "Those ghost rumors have been around for years. They're just crazy stories someone made up. No, my dad and Mr. Steadman have been friends since college. Mr. and Mrs. Steadman called and invited my parents to come for a week, but Mom and Dad couldn't make it. So they invited me and two friends."

"I'm looking forward to doing absolutely nothing but having fun," Nancy admitted.

"Well, you deserve a rest!" Bess said, thumping Nancy on the shoulder. "You've been jumping from one case to the next for a long time. It exhausts me just to think about all the detective work you've done lately!"

Nancy gazed out at the forested hills that surrounded them. The wind rushed through the open window, snatched at her reddish blond hair, and whirled it around her shoulders. "Upstate New York is really beautiful," she commented. "Just look—green as far as the eye can see."

"But what about these ghosts?" Bess pressed. "Is the Steadman Resort really haunted?"

"No," George said, tying a blue bandanna around her short, curly hair to keep it from blowing in the breeze. "But there is an island in the lake—Horse Island—that people say is haunted. Of course, it's not."

"There was a drowning in the lake years ago," Nancy said. "Isn't that what you told me, George?"

George nodded and said, "Several people have claimed to have seen the ghosts of the drowning victims out near the island."

Bess shivered and then sat back in her seat again, folding her arms. "I'm not even going to *think* about ghosts. All I want to do is rest, eat, and get a tan."

"Good idea," Nancy agreed, her blue eyes smiling at Bess in the rearview mirror.

"We're almost there," George said, consulting her map.

"Look, there's a sign," Nancy said, slowing the car. "'Steadman Resort on Triple Tree Lake.' The arrow points left." Nancy turned onto a narrow dirt road.

"Wow, we're really in the deep woods now," Bess said. She took a breath and let it out with a sigh. "Don't you love the smell of the trees and earth? It smells so—well, healthy or something."

Nancy drove the silver car deeper into the forest. Birch and pine trees loomed tall and thick over the road and allowed only a slight filtering of late afternoon sunlight to sift to the ground. The road was rough and uneven with exposed roots. The car pitched slightly from side to side as it made its way up and over hillocks.

Finally they pulled into a sunny clearing, where a large sign loomed over them: Welcome to the Steadman Resort on Beautiful Triple Tree Lake.

"All right!" cried Bess. "It was a long drive, but we made it!"

They rounded a bend, and the lake, blue and crystal clear, came into view. "Oh, man, the lake is beautiful!" George exclaimed. "Anyone for a swim?"

Nancy laughed. "Hold on, George. We've got to check in at the lodge and find our cottage and unpack—"

"And don't forget food!" Bess added. "By the time we get all that done, we'll be ready for dinner!"

George grinned and held up her hands in defeat. "Okay, okay, I give up," she said. "Hey, there's the lodge and dining room," she pointed out as she read the sign on a large log building up ahead. Rattan furniture was positioned on the porch that wrapped around the lodge, and several guests were relaxing there in the shade. Nancy parked the car, and the girls piled out and stretched their stiff muscles.

"Well, this must be George Fayne!" a voice called out. "The same short, curly brown hair and brown eyes I remember when she was a baby."

A balding, portly man dressed in tan slacks and a blue knit shirt walked toward them with a big smile on his face.

"Mr. Steadman!" George said. "My dad has shown me pictures of you!"

"Probably from my leaner days," he chuckled. "And call me Henry. Come on inside. Ruth is working at the desk."

Henry held the door open as the girls trooped into the lodge. The registration desk was just inside the entrance. Beyond it was a lounge with comfortable sofas and dark wood tables strewn with magazines. A large stone fireplace took up the far wall. The room smelled of wood and good food. To the left was the entrance to the dining room, and the girls could see attractively set tables in front of large picture windows that overlooked the lake.

A petite, dark-haired woman stood behind the tall registration desk.

"Ruth, little George Fayne is here!" Henry announced to his wife.

Tall, athletic George laughed. "Not so little anymore," she said, and she shook hands with the smiling woman.

Ruth Steadman greeted her warmly. "George, we're sorry your mom and dad couldn't make it, but we're so pleased that *you* came."

"Henry and Ruth, this is my cousin Bess Marvin and my good friend Nancy Drew," George said.

"Good to meet you, girls," Henry said.

Ruth nodded and said, "We've put you in cottage seventeen, which is down the road a little and right next to the lake. I think you'll like it."

"We love it already," said George. "It's beautiful here."

"Good!" Henry boomed. "That's what we like to hear."

"Just as long as we don't run into any ghosts," Bess said lightly. "People I like; ghosts I don't care for."

Henry and Ruth Steadman glanced worriedly at each other, and Nancy was immediately curious.

"Nancy is a well-known detective, you know,"

Bess continued. "Hanging around with her has gotten us into some pretty scary situations."

"Yes," Henry said, turning to Nancy. "I've heard of your talent for solving mysteries, Ms. Drew. It's exciting to meet someone with your reputation."

"Thank you," Nancy said modestly.

"There really aren't ghosts here, are there?" Bess asked, trying in vain to keep her voice casual.

Henry forced a smile. "There have been stories about ghosts on Horse Island for a long time," he admitted. "But I certainly don't believe in ghosts, do you?"

"Well, not exactly," Bess said. "That is, I've never personally seen a real ghost, and I was hoping I never would."

"I'm sure we won't see any ghosts," Nancy reassured Bess. She wished she knew why the Steadmans seemed so nervous. Surely they didn't believe that the island was haunted. "We've come to relax and enjoy the beautiful scenery."

"Well, you've come to the right place," Henry said. "Have a good week, and don't be strangers. Are you going to eat your meals here at the lodge or cook in your cottage?"

"We'll probably eat here," George said.

"The special tonight is fried chicken," Ruth

7

told them. "Otis, our cook, fixes it so crunchy and tender that it melts in your mouth."

"Oh, stop," Bess wailed, "or I'll drag you all into the dining room right now!"

Everyone laughed.

"Mr. Steadman, I was—" Nancy started to say.

"Please, call me Henry," the man said. "And call my wife Ruth."

"Thank you," said Nancy. "I've been wondering about the name of the lake. Triple Tree? There certainly are more than three trees around here! Where did the name come from?"

Henry smiled. "When this area was first settled," he said, "the people named this Triple Tree Lake because there were three tall oaks that stood alone in a small clearing at the far side of the lake. They're no longer there."

"I see," Nancy said. "It's a beautiful lake."

"We feel lucky to be able to live here," Ruth said, slipping her arm through her husband's.

"Well, I hope we see you at dinner," Henry said, handing George the key to cottage seventeen. "Enjoy your stay."

After signing the register, the girls got back in the car. They drove farther down the dirt road and stopped in front of their cottage, a small log cabin at the edge of the lake. The cabin was shaded by tall pines, and the ground was covered with needles from the trees. A small screened-in porch covered the front of the one-story cottage. They climbed out of the car and unloaded their suitcases, a picnic basket, and raincoats. Loaded down with their belongings, they crossed the wooden walkway to the cottage. The porch door was unlocked, and it squeaked on its hinges when Nancy opened it. George unlocked the cabin door and pushed it open.

"This is great!" Nancy said as the girls entered the cottage.

"It sure is," George agreed.

"And all to ourselves!" exclaimed Bess.

To the left of the door was a small kitchenette with a refrigerator, stove, and sink. To their immediate right was a picnic table, and straight ahead was the living area with a couch and several large chairs positioned around a pine coffee table, two standing lamps, another small lamp on an end table, and a huge rag rug on the floor.

"No TV!" Bess cried in dismay.

"We can listen to the crickets," George said, grinning. "And read."

"That sounds great for a change," said Nancy.

"The bedrooms are over here," George said, crossing the room. "There are two rooms with two beds each. How do you want to divide up?"

"George, you snore," Bess said. "I know from experience."

"No, I don't. You just sleep too lightly," George replied.

"Well, how about if you take the bedroom on the left," Bess suggested, "and Nancy and I take the bedroom on the right?"

"Okay," George said, "but I don't snore!"

"Not much!" Bess teased.

"Nancy," George called later from her bedroom as the girls unpacked, "did you notice how the Steadmans looked at each other when Bess mentioned the ghosts?"

"I did," said Nancy. "Something was definitely bothering them."

"What could it be?" George wondered.

"Oh, no, you don't!" said Bess emphatically.

"What?" Nancy and George asked at the same time.

"We're here for rest and relaxation!" Bess told them. "No mysteries, remember?"

Nancy laughed. "That's right, Bess. No mysteries. Just peace and quiet for a whole week!"

Suddenly, from outside the cottage came an ear-shattering scream!

2

Uninvited Guests

Nancy, Bess, and George raced out the door of their cottage.

"Where did that scream come from?" George asked.

Her question was answered when another scream pierced the quiet evening air.

"That cottage over there!" Nancy yelled, running toward the small log building closest to their own. Bess and George followed close behind.

The girls arrived at the cottage in a few seconds. The heavy door was standing open, and the living room was visible through a screen door. The room was in a shambles—furniture overturned, lamps broken, clothes and linens strewn around the floor.

"What happened here?" Bess gasped.

Nancy pounded on the screen door. "Hello?" she called. "Are you all right?"

"Oh, it's awful!" a young woman's voice cried.

"What a mess!" another female voice answered.

Nancy pounded again. "Hello?"

A girl with long, straight, white blond hair peeked out from one of the bedrooms. She was in her late teens, though there was a childlike expression in her large blue eyes. "Oh, come in," she said in a high-pitched voice.

"Are you all right?" asked Nancy, opening the door. She, Bess, and George walked inside.

"*We're* okay," the girl said. "But look what someone did to this place!"

A second girl, a little younger than the first, appeared from the other bedroom. Her curly red hair was caught up in a ponytail at the top of her head. She wore a short purple skirt and a flowered top.

"Why would someone *do* this?" she cried.

"Did you see anyone?" Nancy asked.

"No," the blond girl said, pushing her long bangs from her eyes. "We just got back from the lodge."

12

"We heard screams," George said. "We thought someone was hurt—"

"Oh, that was just my sister, Carrie," the older sister told them. "She screams at everything."

"I do not, Ann!" Carrie protested. "It's a shocking experience to walk into your cottage and see things thrown all over the place!"

"You didn't need to scream," Ann insisted. "Ever since you were a little kid—"

"Was your door locked?" asked Nancy, hoping to distract the girls from their argument.

"No," Ann said.

"We never lock it," said Carrie. "I mean, we never thought we had to here in the woods."

"Is anything missing?" Nancy asked.

"Missing?" Carrie repeated, looking around. "It doesn't look like it. No, I don't think so."

"Did you check for things like jewelry and money?" Nancy asked.

"Well, no, not exactly," Carrie admitted. "I was too busy screaming."

"Why don't you look around?" Nancy suggested. "See if you're missing anything valuable."

"I'd better check my pocketbook," said Ann. She turned and walked into one of the bedrooms. Carrie disappeared into the other bedroom.

13

George looked questioningly at Nancy. Nancy shrugged. The ransacking of the cottage certainly suggested a robbery, but it was strange that the girls didn't think that anything was missing.

"Our money's still here," said Ann, returning from her bedroom with a wallet and showing Nancy that there was plenty of cash inside. "The drawer was sitting in the middle of the room, but the wallet with our salaries in it was still there. Is this weird, or what?"

"Salaries?" Nancy asked. "Are you employed at the resort?"

"Oh, right, sorry," Ann said. "I should've introduced myself. I'm Ann Burkle." Carrie appeared from her room. "This is my sister, Carrie. We sing at the lodge every night after dinner. And we take the guests horseback riding."

"But we're mostly singers," Carrie added. "We're entertainers, and someday we hope to get a recording deal."

Nancy smiled. "Right now we ought to figure out why your cottage was ransacked. We should look for clues. Did the intruder leave anything behind?"

"Like in a mystery novel?" Carrie asked. "What should we look for?"

"What kind of clues?" Ann asked at the same time.

14

"Anything that doesn't belong to you," Nancy said. "Anything the intruder might have dropped."

The sisters began walking slowly around the living room, their heads down as they looked for anything unusual. Nancy, Bess, and George stood at the edges of the room and watched.

A white slip of paper on the picnic table in the kitchen caught Nancy's eye. She stepped over to it. "Here's something!" she exclaimed. "Look!"

"What is it?" Carrie asked as she ran over to the table. She picked it up and turned it over in her hand. "It's a note! It says, 'Get away from this resort immediately or you will be in great danger!'"

Carrie's eyes went wide with horror and she dropped the note. Once again she screamed.

"Will you stop that screaming?" Ann shouted.

"I can't help it," Carrie said. "I am scared to death by this note."

"Can you think of anyone who would send you a threatening note?" Nancy asked.

"No, nobody," Carrie wailed.

"Apparently *somebody* wants us to leave here," said Ann, slumping into a chair.

"Think a minute. Is there anyone *at all* who could have a reason for wanting you to leave the resort?" Nancy prodded.

15

The sisters gazed at each other with bewildered expressions and then shook their heads.

"Let me know if you think of anyone," Nancy said. "I'm sorry this happened to you. I'm Nancy. This is Bess and George. We're right next door if you need help any time this week."

"Thanks for coming over," Ann said. "This really is pretty scary. I just don't understand it."

"Well, you should probably be careful for the next few days," Nancy said. "It could have been a prank, but just in case someone means business, you'd better be sure to lock your door."

"We will," Ann said.

"You can bet on that," Carrie agreed. "And be sure to come to our show. We have tonight off, though."

"What time do you usually go on?" Nancy asked.

"At seven-thirty," Carrie said. "Sharp. Henry doesn't like us to be late even one minute."

The girls said goodbye and returned to their cottage.

"What an excitable girl Carrie is," Bess said.

"She certainly is a character," Nancy agreed, "although finding your cabin ransacked is a horrible experience. And that threatening note would scare anyone."

16

"I hope they aren't bothered anymore," George said.

"So do I. Let's change for dinner and then take a walk around the resort," Nancy suggested. "I'd like to see what's here."

"Good idea," George agreed.

"Yeah," said Bess. "I especially like the dinner part. I'm starved!"

The girls changed from shorts to casual skirts and blouses and took a walking tour of the resort. The early evening sun was low in the sky, and the air was scented with the aroma of the nearby pine forest. Other guests, mostly couples and families, were out walking, heading toward the lodge for dinner. Their cheerful voices carried on the light breeze off the lake.

"This place has everything!" Nancy exclaimed. "A lake with a private dock and motorboat for each cottage, a heated swimming pool, stables for horseback riding, tennis courts—"

"A recreation cabin," George chimed in, "and an archery field—"

"And a dining room with *food!*" Bess said. "Let's eat!"

"I'm for that," said George.

"This resort is famous for its good food," George told Bess and Nancy as the girls headed

17

toward the lodge. "Dad said people come back year after year just for the meals at the lodge."

"This is going to be a terrific week, then," Bess said heartily.

They arrived at the restaurant, and the hostess led the girls to their table, next to a window overlooking the lake. They all ordered the night's special, fried chicken.

Their waitress, a young woman wearing a name tag that said Margie, smiled. "You'll love it," she said. "It's better than any fried chicken you've ever tasted."

"Great!" Bess said.

"Say, maybe you can tell us," Nancy said to Margie. "We're interested in the two singers, Ann and Carrie Burkle."

Margie smiled. "Have you seen them perform?" Nancy shook her head. "They sing very well," Margie said. "And they're pretty funny. I don't think they mean to be funny, though."

"Are they friends of yours?" Nancy asked.

"Well, we're not close or anything," Margie said. "But everybody likes them." She eyed Nancy curiously. "Why do you ask?"

"Oh, no reason," Nancy said. "We just met them this afternoon, and they seemed very nice."

Margie smiled cheerfully. "Yeah, they are. Well, I'd better get this order in for you."

"Looking for the sisters' enemies?" George asked Nancy after Margie had left.

"I guess," Nancy said. "They just don't seem like the type of girls who would cultivate enemies."

"I know what you mean," said George.

"No, they don't," Bess added.

A woman and a man holding a little boy's hand came in and seated themselves at the next table. "But, Mommy, I don't want to leave!" the boy wailed.

"Honey, our reservations are for three more days," the man pleaded with his wife.

"Well, I just feel too nervous here," the woman insisted. "Those bloodcurdling screams this afternoon! That was the final straw!"

Nancy and the girls looked at one another.

"Excuse me," Nancy said, leaning over toward the family. "We couldn't help overhearing. I can explain those screams this afternoon—"

"What on earth was going on?" the woman demanded.

"Two members of the staff had their cottage ransacked," Nancy explained. "But nothing was taken." Nancy felt there was no reason to tell the family about the threatening note. "It could have been just a mean prank," she added.

"*Ransacked?*" the woman said. "That's it! We're leaving!"

"Honey," the man said.

"But, Mom——" the boy cried.

"No buts!" his mother said. "We're leaving! This place is too scary!"

"You mean there've been other things going on?" Nancy asked.

"You'd better believe it!" the woman told her. "Yesterday, my husband found a *live snake* in his tackle box! He had shut it tight the night before and left it in the boat. Someone obviously put it there during the night!"

"Was it——" Bess began.

"No, it wasn't poisonous," said the woman, "but *we* didn't know that! There *are* poisonous snakes in the area. I nearly had a heart attack!"

"Maybe it was a joke," George said.

"Some joke!" the woman huffed indignantly.

"Yes, there *are* strange things going on," a voice chimed in from the other side of the girls' table. They turned to see a middle-aged man and his wife, who had been following the conversation. "Someone's been prowling around our cottage at night, tapping on the windows."

"Did you investigate?" Nancy asked.

"Of course," the man said. "And we called the Steadmans, even though the tapping occurred twice in the middle of the night. But by the time Henry Steadman arrived—both times—the person was gone."

The man's wife leaned over. "I know that tapping on the window doesn't sound terribly dangerous, but let me tell you, when you're awakened in the dead of night by someone standing out in the darkness—"

"Oh, that sounds scary enough to me!" Bess said with a shiver of fear in her voice.

"See what I mean?" the first woman said, nodding. "That's why we're leaving. I'm not going to wait until something *really* bad happens and someone gets hurt."

"What does Mr. Steadman say about all this?" Nancy asked. "He must be very concerned." Now Henry's worried glances at his wife made sense to Nancy.

"He's more concerned about his pocketbook," the first woman said. "He's afraid all the guests will leave. And that's exactly what we're going to do!"

"Are you leaving, too?" Nancy asked, turning to the older couple.

"No," the man said. "At least not yet. I don't want to let some jokester scare me out of my vacation."

21

"Good," Nancy said. "I'm sure these things will end, or we'll find out who's behind them."

Margie brought the girls' salads, and the other diners began talking among themselves.

"Margie," Nancy said, "we've just been hearing about some strange things going on here. Have you heard about them?"

Margie's mouth tightened into a thin line. She lowered her voice. "I know what you're talking about," she said, "but the staff has been given strict orders not to discuss it with the guests."

"Has anything happened to you?" Nancy whispered.

"No," Margie said. "And I'm hoping nothing will."

"Is this your first summer working here?" Nancy asked her.

"No, it's my third, and nothing weird ever happened here before this," said Margie. She hurried off to wait on another table.

Bess shivered. "I thought this was going to be a relaxing week."

"Me, too," said George. "But it's a shame the Steadmans are having so much trouble here."

"Yes, it is," Nancy agreed. "Let's talk to them later."

After dinner the girls found Henry Steadman

22

behind the registration desk. "Henry, could we talk to you?" George asked.

"Of course," said Henry, a worry line creasing his wide brow. The girls huddled around the desk. Fortunately, no other guests were within earshot.

"Henry," George said, lowering her voice, "we've been hearing about some pretty weird things going on here. What's happening?"

"I don't know," Henry said seriously. "I wish I did. Ruth and I have been here for twenty years, and nothing like this has ever happened before."

"Do you have any reason to think that someone might be angry with you?" Nancy asked.

Henry shook his head. "I mean, everyone has arguments occasionally with people, but I can't think of anyone who would want to hurt me or my wife."

"We overheard one of your guests say that she and her family are leaving," George told him.

Henry nodded. "The incident with the snake. I can understand why that would upset her."

"Another couple told us they've had prowlers," Nancy said.

"And now the Burkle sisters!" Bess said.

"What?" cried Henry, surprised. "What happened to the girls?"

"Their cottage was ransacked," Nancy said. "Nothing was taken, but they were pretty upset." Nancy told Henry about the note and that Ann and Carrie had no idea who could have written it.

"They didn't tell me," Henry said. He shook his head. "I don't know what to do."

"Why don't you have Nancy investigate?" George proposed. "You won't find a better detective anywhere."

Henry looked up hopefully. "Would you, Nancy?" he asked. "I know you came here for a relaxing week, but if you could—"

"I'd be happy to," Nancy assured him. "We'll have a good week, and in the meantime, I'll nose around and see what I can find out."

Henry's worried expression faded a bit. "Thank you, Nancy," he said. "I really would appreciate anything you could do."

"Don't worry," George said. "If anyone can find out what's going on, Nancy can."

The girls left the lodge and walked toward their cottage.

"I just hope these weird things aren't the work of a ghost," Bess said. "Maybe it wants the lake to itself and it's trying to scare people away!"

"I doubt that." Nancy laughed. "A snake in a tackle box and a ransacked cottage sound like the work of human beings to me."

"It's hard to believe all this could be going on at such a peaceful place," said George.

The girls stopped at their cottage door, and George pulled the key out of her pocket.

Just then a loud crash came from inside their cottage!

3

Island Lore

"Quick!" said Nancy. "Let's catch them in the act!"

George shoved open the unlocked door. Nancy and George sprang into the room with Bess right behind.

"Anything in your room?" Nancy called to George, who had charged into her bedroom.

"The screen is unlocked and open," George hollered back.

Nancy ran into the bedroom she was sharing with Bess. Nothing was disturbed.

At that moment Bess let out a shriek in the living room. Nancy and George raced out of the bedrooms.

"What is it?" Nancy cried out.

Bess stood frozen next to the door. She pointed slowly into the kitchen.

Nancy ran to the kitchen and stopped dead in her tracks.

There on the countertop sat a fat raccoon. The girls had left their picnic basket out, and the raccoon was helping itself to an apple left over from their lunch. The basket was tipped over on the counter, and three empty soda cans had landed on the kitchen floor.

"Oh!" gasped Bess, walking to the kitchen. "I had no idea raccoons were so big!"

"They have sharp claws, too," added George, joining them. "Don't get too close."

The raccoon had backed into a corner behind a toaster, a trapped, frightened look in its eyes.

Nancy, Bess, and George stepped out of the kitchen. "What do we do now?" asked Bess.

"I have an idea," said Nancy. She grabbed her knapsack off the table and took out a small bag of pretzels. "Maybe this will appeal to him," she said, tearing open the cellophane bag. Nancy walked into the kitchen and lifted the screen in the window over the sink.

Then Bess and George followed Nancy out the door and around to the kitchen window. Standing on her tiptoes, Nancy placed one pretzel on the windowsill. The raccoon eyed it cautiously. Nancy dropped another pretzel on the ground below it, making a trail of pretzels leading away from the cabin.

The girls stood off to one side of the cabin and watched as the raccoon poked its head out the window and grabbed the first pretzel. Then it scrambled down the side of the cabin after the remaining pretzels.

Quickly Nancy, Bess, and George ran back into the cabin. Bess slammed down the kitchen screen. "Boy, raccoons look so adorable in picture books, but they're a little scary in person."

George laughed. "That's my cousin, a real country girl."

"They *are* bigger than you think," said Nancy, smiling. "I'm glad we could lure him out. Henry has enough problems right now without worrying about getting rid of a raccoon."

"Do you think the raccoon could have been the culprit in the Burkle sisters' cottage?" asked George.

Nancy shook her head. "The note. Remember?"

"That's right. How could I forget that note?" said George, dropping down into one of the living room chairs.

"How do you think the raccoon got in?" Bess asked, looking around a little nervously.

"Probably my bedroom window," George said. "There's a tree right outside it, and I'm sure the raccoon could have climbed up it and then gotten in through the window."

"We'd better be more careful about locking this place up," Bess said, "with all that's been happening around here."

Bess stretched out on the couch. "I don't know about you guys," she said, "but I've had enough thrills for one day. I'm going to bed early."

"Good idea," agreed Nancy, kicking off her sneakers. "I have the feeling we have a big day ahead of us tomorrow."

"I haven't canoed in a long time," said George the next morning as the girls neared the boat house on the lake. "This will be great." They had risen early, eaten a breakfast of waffles and strawberries at the lodge, and signed up for the guided canoe trip.

"We'll get a chance to see more of the area," Nancy said. "Maybe we'll even get a look at Horse Island."

"Please," groaned Bess. "Do we have to go *looking* for ghosts?"

As the girls laughed, a handsome man in his

late twenties approached them from the dock. His dark blond hair fluttered in the light breeze off the lake. A pair of sunglasses was perched on his nose. "Hello, ladies," he greeted them.

"Hi," they responded.

"Here for the canoe trip?" he asked.

"Yep," said Bess pertly.

"Great. I'm Steve Matheson, the Steadmans' activities director. I'll be your guide."

After introducing themselves, Nancy, Bess, and George followed Steve down to the dock. Other guests soon arrived for the trip. The first to show up were a young couple, Jeff and Cindy. They announced almost immediately that they were on their honeymoon. Then came the older couple who'd spoken to Nancy and the girls about the prowler at their window. They introduced themselves as Mr. and Mrs. Savage. Last to arrive was the Mathew family, a man and woman and their two little girls: Heather, who was nine years old, and Jessica, who was two years younger.

"Okay," said Steve, consulting his sign-up sheet. "We're all here. Who knows how to handle the stern of a canoe?"

"The what?" asked Jessica.

"I guess that means you don't." Steve chuckled. "The canoe is steered from the stern. That's a fancy way of saying the back of the boat. You need to know how to do what we call a J-stroke to keep the boat on course."

George raised her hand. She'd gone on many canoeing trips and was expert at handling a boat. Nancy also knew how to handle an oar. So did Mr. Mathew, Mrs. Savage, and Jeff.

"Super," said Steve. "We have a pilot for each group. The canoes are stacked in the boat house. So are the life jackets. Let's get going."

Soon the boats were all in the water, and the group was paddling out onto the lake. "I forgot my suntan oil," Bess said from her seat in the middle of the canoe between George and Nancy.

"Forget the oil and use the sunblock I threw into the canoe next to you," cautioned George. "These aluminum canoes are like reflectors for the sun. You can get fried out here."

"Oh, thanks," said Bess.

Steve led the group along the shoreline, around a bend, and into a small cove. "Hold up here," he called, raising his tanned arm. The canoers pulled up next to one another, and Steve turned his canoe so that he was facing them.

"Look sharp and you may see some deer along the shore," he told them. "We also have foxes and skunks—"

"Not to mention raccoons," George said, and Nancy and Bess chuckled.

"What about the horses?" asked Heather Mathew.

"What horses?" Steve asked.

Heather pointed to the island about a mile off in the middle of the lake. "Isn't that Horse Island?"

Steve nodded. "There used to be wild horses living there," he explained, "but they were removed and tamed years ago."

"Oh," the girl said glumly. "You mean there are no wild horses there anymore?"

"I'm afraid not," Steve told her.

Bess asked the question that had been on her mind since they had arrived. "I hear the island is haunted," she said with a nervous laugh. "I don't suppose there's any truth to those stories, is there?"

"We heard that, too," Cindy said, glancing at her new husband. Then she turned back to Steve. "Have you ever seen ghosts near there?"

"No, I can't say that I have," he said, smiling. Then he grew serious and gazed at each of the guests individually. "But Horse Island is off-limits to the guests at the resort," he told them. "And there is a very good reason for that. Even though hunting is illegal at this time of year, there are people who go to the island every summer and kill wildlife. These people are irresponsible with their weapons and act as if they're having a big party. A couple of years ago, three Steadman guests decided to explore the island, and two of them were accidentally shot by careless hunters."

The guests gasped.

"Did they die?" Mrs. Savage asked anxiously.

"No, but they nearly did," Steve said.

"You couldn't get me near the place," Cindy said nervously.

"Yeah, we won't go there," Bess agreed, obviously relieved that she wouldn't have to go to the island.

"How did Horse Island get the reputation of being haunted?" Mr. Savage asked.

"That's an interesting story," Steve said. "About fifty years ago, a wealthy New York financier built a summer home on the island. He and his wife lived there off and on for about ten years. But one summer evening their boat capsized in the lake during a storm, and they were drowned."

"And people say the man and his wife are still wandering on their island?" Bess asked anxiously.

"Well, that's what some folks say," Steve said. "Several people have reported seeing the ghosts of the couple. Usually on dark, rainy nights."

Bess shivered. "Let's talk about something else," she said. "This conversation is giving me the creeps. Besides, these kids shouldn't hear scary stories."

"No, tell us more about the haunted island," Jessica Mathew pleaded. "It's awesome!"

"Kids are used to this stuff," Mrs. Mathew explained to the laughing group. "TV, you know."

"That's about all there is to tell," Steve said to the little girls. "But as I said earlier, you should all stay away from the island. Those hunters don't care *what* they're aiming at! In fact, occasionally you can hear gunshots from the island. Then you know there are hunters in the area."

"Why doesn't the local sheriff go in there and arrest them?" Nancy asked.

Steve shrugged. "He's been called to the island several times," he said. "But the poachers are always gone by the time he gets there."

"Well, can we paddle close enough to the island to see the financier's summer home?" Jeff asked. "Is it still standing?"

"Oh, Jeff, let's stay away from there," Cindy said with a shiver.

"The house is still there," Steve said, "but all we'd see would be the roof. It's back a ways from shore." He paused a moment. "We'll get a little closer, but not much. I wouldn't want any stray bullets flying our way!''

Following Steve's lead, the group paddled out toward the island. When they were about a quarter of a mile from the shoreline, Steve once again signaled for them to stop.

"Could a bullet shot from a rifle reach us?" Cindy asked her husband. Nancy could hear their conversation from her canoe, which George had pulled up beside Cindy and Jeff's.

"I doubt it," Jeff said. "But I don't think Steve would let us get that close."

Almost before the words were out of his mouth, a shot rang out from the island.

"Someone's shooting at us!" screamed Cindy, frantically getting to her feet. "We have to get out of here!"

"Cindy, sit down!" Jeff cried as he reached out for her.

But Cindy, in her panic, dropped her paddle in the water. She bent over to try to retrieve it, and her sudden movement rocked the canoe on its side. She lost her balance, and in an instant, both she and her husband toppled into the water!

Cindy quickly rose to the surface. Her arms thrashed the water wildly. "I can't swim!" she screamed.

4

Horsing Around

In a flash Nancy extended her oar to Cindy. "Grab on to this," she called. "Your life jacket will keep you up." Cindy threw herself at the oar. Her weight rocked Nancy's canoe.

"Keep your weight low," George cautioned. She leaned to the side to keep the canoe from tipping as Bess and Nancy helped Cindy into the canoe.

"Where's Jeff?" called Nancy, once Cindy was seated next to Bess.

"Jeff!" Cindy shrieked.

"I'm here," he panted, coming up on the side of his canoe. Luckily their boat had righted itself—after tossing out its passengers.

In the next moment, Steve paddled alongside

the canoe. "Here, let me help you." Steve leaned out of his canoe and put his weight on the bow while Jeff climbed in over the stern.

"Everything okay now?" Steve asked.

Jeff and Cindy nodded, but it was clear they both were shaken. Steve retrieved their floating paddles, Cindy rejoined her husband in their canoe, and soon the group was heading back to the resort.

"It's a shame that some greedy poachers are preventing others from exploring the island," Nancy said as she, Bess, and George were walking away from the boat house.

"Uh-oh, Nancy, I don't like that look in your eye," said Bess. "You always have that look when you're about to do something dangerous."

Nancy smiled. "No, I'm not planning anything right now," she said. "Let's sit tight for the time being and see what develops."

The girls headed toward the lodge for a light lunch. While they were eating, Ann and Carrie walked into the dining room and over to the grand piano at the edge of the room.

They opened the piano bench, left several sheets of music, and turned to leave. Carrie saw Nancy and the girls at their table and waved. The girls waved back as Carrie and Ann approached the table.

"We've calmed down since we last saw you," Ann said somewhat sheepishly, nodding at her sister. "No more screaming."

Nancy had to smile.

"What have you been up to?" Ann asked.

"We took a canoe ride this morning," Nancy told her.

"Oh, with Steve Matheson?" asked Carrie. Nancy nodded, and Carrie continued. "He's adorable, don't you think? I mean, he's way too old for me, but I can still *look*, right?" She raced right on. "Oh, and speaking of cute, wait till you see Rodney Starr, the stable guy. He's closer to my age, so I'm zeroing in on him this summer!"

"The stable guy?" Nancy asked.

"Yeah, he takes care of the horses," Carrie replied.

"He may not be working here much longer, though," Ann said.

"Why not?" Nancy inquired.

"He wants to make more money. He says the Steadmans don't pay him enough," Ann replied.

"Oh?" Nancy glanced at Bess and George and, with a flick of her eyebrow, let them know they should let the sisters do the talking.

"Yeah," Carrie said. "They should pay us more, too."

"Do the other staff members feel the same?" asked Nancy.

"Well, we'll never get rich working here," Ann said. "That's for sure. Everyone complains. Especially Otis. You should hear him moan and groan about his salary."

"He's the cook, isn't he?" Nancy recalled.

"The *chef!*" Carrie corrected Nancy. "If he heard you call him a mere cook, he'd have a fit."

"Yes, Otis considers himself an artist," added Ann.

"If you ask me, Otis is just a crabby old guy," said Carrie. "He gets mad about everything. But especially his salary."

"Who else doesn't like the Steadmans?" Nancy asked casually. She hoped the Burkle sisters would suggest some possible suspects. "They seem like nice people to me."

"Oh, they're really not bad," Ann said. "But, you know, people are funny sometimes. Speaking of funny, have you met that newlywed couple who is staying here?"

"Cindy and Jeff?" George said.

"Right," said Ann. "What a pair of lovebirds! I love to watch them!"

"Yeah," Carrie said, laughing. "What a hoot! They're always holding hands and staring into each other's eyes."

"And you should check out that woman in cottage fourteen," Ann said, flipping her long hair over her shoulder.

"Yeah, she's so mysterious," Carrie said.

"What's mysterious about her?" Nancy asked.

"Nobody knows *anything* about her," Carrie said. "She's here all by herself. Isn't that strange?"

"It might be nice to be alone," said Ann. "It sure sounds good to me."

"Meaning what?" Carrie said, her hands on her hips.

"Just what I said," Ann snapped, her voice growing louder. "I'd sure like—"

"Well, I think this place is great for a vacation," Nancy cut in, hoping to stop the impending argument.

"Me, too," George said. "Bess, are you finished with lunch? I want to sign up for the horseback ride."

"Oh, we're guiding this afternoon's ride," Carrie told them. "You'll be with us!"

"Oh, great," George said. "I forgot you two did that."

"Yeah, and you can meet Rodney Starr," Carrie said.

Nancy, Bess, and George excused themselves to go back to their cottage. "Did you get any clues from that talk with the Burkles?" Bess asked Nancy.

"I'm not sure," Nancy confessed as they passed the back of the dining lodge. "I'd like to know more about Otis, though."

George nudged Nancy and pointed to a large man with a full head of snow-white hair trudging up the back stairs leading to the kitchen. He wore a white apron and carried a covered tray. "Maybe that's Otis," she said.

"Let's find out," said Nancy, hurrying toward the man.

"What do you plan to say?" Bess asked, following her.

"I'll say I'm a big fan of his cooking," said Nancy, not slowing her pace. She bounded up the wooden steps and was about to pull open the screen door when something stopped her. It was the sound of a raised voice.

Signaling George and Bess to stay back, Nancy cautiously leaned toward the screen to observe the scene. The man they thought was Otis was angrily stomping back and forth as he ranted.

"I've got half a notion to put the Steadmans completely out of business," he told a young man dressed in a white cook's suit. "It wouldn't be hard to do, you know! I could do it like that!"

He pounded a butcher block counter angrily

with his fist. The young assistant hung back, looking nervous.

"They promised me a raise, and this is what they come up with?" the older man cried, waving an envelope.

"Should I start the clam chowder, Otis?" the young man asked timidly.

"It's crab bisque tonight!" shouted Otis. "And do you mean to tell me you haven't started it yet?"

As Otis continued his tirade, Nancy slipped away from the door and moved down the stairs.

"That was certainly an earful," said Bess. "We could hear him down here at the bottom of the steps."

"That guy has definitely made it onto my suspect list," Nancy told her friends.

The girls returned to their cottage and changed into jeans and cotton blouses. The sun was high in the sky, and the day was warming up.

"A great day to ride," George said as the girls walked down to the stables at the end of the road. Several teenagers, two girls and a boy, were waiting for the horse ride to begin, along with the Mathew family. The Burkle sisters were already there, leading horses out of the wooden stable. A young man with light blond hair and bright blue eyes seemed to be in charge of the horses. He was

42

saddling the animals, selecting the right horse for the right rider.

"This is Rodney Starr," Carrie said to the girls. "I told you about him, remember? He's the horse expert around here."

The girls nodded and said hello.

"Here's a pony for you," Rodney said to Heather Mathew. "I think we'll put your sister on the same horse with your daddy."

"Good idea," said Mr. Mathew as Rodney led out a gentle gray mare.

The Burkles and Rodney helped the inexperienced riders mount their horses. Nancy noted that the sisters seemed to be very confident horsewomen.

"Inexperienced riders should be up front behind Carrie," Ann instructed the group. "Experienced riders stay to the back of the line. I'll take up the end."

"I guess I'll go up front," said Bess, who hadn't ridden much. Nancy and George had ridden many times, so they stayed back with Ann.

"Where did you two learn to ride?" Nancy asked Ann.

"We grew up on a horse ranch in Wyoming," said Ann. "Riding is second nature to us."

Nancy filed the information. Maybe there were other things she would discover about the sisters as time went on. She'd have to suspect everyone who worked at the resort until she learned more about all of its employees.

"Are you riding?" Nancy asked Rodney Starr, who walked down the line checking everyone's saddle and stirrups for proper fit.

"No, ma'am, not today," he replied. "I guide three days a week. The girls guide the other four. I have another job in town."

"Okay, let's move out," Carrie called from the head of the line.

The group, in a single line, clopped along the trail leading away from the stable. Carrie led the riders out into an open meadow along a gently rolling hillside. The view was a spectacle of color: the heavily wooded, deep green shades of the hills and, behind them, a cloudless blue sky.

They crossed the meadow and came to the edge of a dense forest.

"Stay in a single line," Carrie called back to the guests as her horse stepped into the woods.

"I think my horse likes me, Mom," Heather Mathew said over her shoulder.

"These do seem like nice, gentle animals," her mother answered.

The top branches of the trees filtered out much

of the sun's brightness, and the forest grew considerably darker as the riders headed into it.

"It's kind of spooky in here," Jessica said. She leaned back into her father, who was riding with her on the light gray horse.

"There's nothing to be afraid of," Mr. Mathew assured the little girl.

The riders followed a sharp curve in the path and entered a small clearing.

"What's that?" Heather cried suddenly, pointing into the clearing.

The riders came to an abrupt halt, stunned by the sight before them.

There, hanging from a branch on the one tree in the middle of the clearing, was a figure dangling from a rope.

5

Ghost Stories

Carrie let out a scream that startled several birds in the surrounding trees. There was a rustling of leaves and the sound of wings flapping as the birds flew away.

"Someone hanged himself!" gasped Ann.

Jessica Mathew began to cry. "I want to go," she whimpered, turning her head into her father's chest.

Summoning up all her nerve, Nancy galloped out into the clearing. She had to see who was hanging from that branch. The body was turned away from her. She could see only its back. It appeared to be a man in tan slacks and a blue shirt.

As the body dangled lifelessly, a gentle breeze swung it around to face Nancy. Her heart leapt into her throat. Whom would she find at the end of that rope?

"Wait a minute," Nancy murmured after taking a second look at the dangling figure. She was now close enough to realize what she was looking at. "It's a dummy!" she said aloud.

It was a mannequin, the kind used in department stores. And there was a note taped to its forehead. Nancy rode up to the dummy and pulled down the paper.

"What does it say?" asked George, pulling her horse up alongside Nancy's.

Nancy handed her the note. " 'Get away from the Steadman Resort,' " George read. " 'Your life is in danger.' "

"Some joke, huh?" Nancy said glumly.

"Whoever is responsible for this is starting to seem more and more twisted," commented George, handing the note back to Nancy.

George leaned forward in her saddle and lifted the noose over the dummy's neck. The mannequin fell to the ground with a thud. "Is it a clue?" she asked Nancy. "Should we take it back with us?"

Nancy studied the stiff figure on the ground. "Leave it," she said. "I won't forget what it looks

47

like." The two girls turned and rode back to the group.

"It's only a prank," Nancy told the anxious riders. "That's just a dummy out there."

"We saw you reading something," said Mrs. Mathew.

Nancy hesitated, then decided she owed it to the other guests to tell them the truth. "It was a warning to leave the resort," she admitted.

"That's it!" said Mrs. Mathew. "It's time to start packing."

"I want to go home!" cried her youngest daughter, sensing the horror of the riders but not really understanding what was going on.

"Now, folks," said Ann, trying in vain to use a soothing tone of voice, "I'm sure this is all harmless."

"Well, it's one too many of the silly pranks that have been going on around here," said Mr. Mathew. "This one is in horribly bad taste."

"I agree," said one of the teenage girls, her face ashen.

"Ann and Carrie," Nancy spoke up, "I think we should return to the stables now."

"I think you're right," Ann said. "Come on, folks, turn your horses by pulling the reins to your right."

The group turned and headed back to the stables. At a turn in the trail, Nancy caught sight of a woman who stood watching them from behind some trees. She was large-boned and athletic. Nancy guessed her age to be around thirty. Her hair was dark, shoulder length, and turned under at the ends. She seemed to study the riders as if memorizing each face.

When her gaze fixed on Nancy, Nancy stared straight back. A look of alarm passed over the woman's face, and she turned abruptly and disappeared behind the stand of trees.

Who was she? Nancy wondered. Was it just a coincidence that she was watching the group of riders that had just found the dummy hanging in the woods?

Nancy beckoned to Bess and George after they had dismounted at the stables. She led them away to a spot out of earshot of the others.

"Did you see the woman watching us?" Nancy whispered urgently.

"I did," George said. "Do you think she planted the dummy to scare us?"

"I don't know," said Nancy. "Let's find her and see what she has to say. Come on!"

"I didn't see her," Bess said. "What did she look like?"

Nancy described the woman. "And she was wearing a pair of jeans and a light blue sleeveless blouse. Right, George?"

"Right," George agreed. The girls took off on foot in the direction the woman had taken.

"She's probably a guest," Nancy said. "Otherwise she'd have been working—unless this is her day off."

"Maybe she turned back to the lane toward the cottages," George suggested.

"Let's try it," Nancy said.

The girls hurried around to the lane.

"There she is!" Nancy said in a low voice as she pointed to the woman, who was walking along the lane ahead of them at a quick pace. "Let's hurry and catch up, but don't run unless she takes off."

The girls hurried to shorten the woman's lead. When they were about a hundred feet from her, she turned and, seeing the girls behind her, quickly ducked in between two cottages.

"Let's follow her," Nancy said.

The girls rushed to the spot where the woman had stepped off the lane. She was not between the cottages.

"She must have come around the side to lose us," Nancy said. "Let's keep looking. George, you and Bess go around to the left. I'll take the right."

Nancy and the girls separated to search. Nancy slowed her pace—the woman surely was not far away. Nancy came around the front of a cottage that faced the lake. The woman was standing motionless among a group of pine trees that grew close to the water's edge.

"Hi," Nancy said, trying to sound casual.

The woman turned and looked at Nancy as if she'd never seen her before. "Hello," she said, her face an unsmiling mask.

"Are you a guest here?" Nancy asked.

"Of course I'm a guest!" the woman said impatiently. "Aren't we all guests here?"

"I mean you're not staff," Nancy said calmly.

The woman looked at her watch, turned abruptly, and headed away toward a group of cottages without saying another word.

Nancy stepped into the lane and watched her go. The woman stopped at the door of cottage fourteen, took out a key, and disappeared inside.

Just then Bess and George appeared. "We didn't find her," said George breathlessly. "You have any luck?"

"Not much," Nancy said. "I talked to her, but she made it very plain that she had no interest in talking to me."

"Is she a guest?" Bess asked.

"That much I did learn," Nancy said. "She

said she was a guest and went into cottage fourteen. She must be the mysterious woman the Burkle sisters told us about."

"But what was she doing watching us come back from the horseback ride?" George wondered aloud.

"I don't know," said Nancy.

George looked around her. "I wonder where the division is between guest and staff cottages," she said.

"It would have to be right after ours," Nancy pointed out. "Remember, the Burkle sisters live in cottage eighteen, next to us."

"Some of the staff must live in town," George noted.

"Right," Nancy said. "Rodney Starr said he had a job in town, so I'll bet he lives around here all year."

"Well, I don't know about you two, but I'm up for a break in investigating and a dip in the pool," George said. "How about it?"

"Just let me grab my tanning lotion," Bess said.

"You two go ahead," said Nancy. "I think I'll have a little talk with Henry about his guest in cottage fourteen. No doubt he's already heard about the dummy hanging in the woods. I want to see what he has to say about that, too."

"Meet us at the pool when you're done," George said.

"Okay," said Nancy. "I'll be there in a half hour."

Bess and George headed for the cottage, and Nancy turned back toward the lodge. She found Henry Steadman visiting with some guests in the lobby of the lodge. When he saw Nancy, he excused himself and approached her.

"Hello, Nancy," he said. He leaned in toward Nancy and lowered his voice. "Did you hear about what happened along the riding trail this afternoon?"

"Yes," Nancy said. "I was there."

"Another family left because of that."

"The Mathews, right?" Nancy said.

Henry nodded. "I don't know what I'm going to do. That's four groups of guests we've lost in the last three weeks! And everyone else seems nervous. I've had at least a dozen people approach me to ask what in blazes is going on here."

"Henry," Nancy said, "there was a woman near the stables. She's a guest in cottage number fourteen. Do you know her?"

"Teresa Diamond," Henry said. "She arrived three days ago, and she's staying for ten days."

"Do you know anything more about her?"

"Nope, just her name and home address," replied Henry.

"Where does she live?" Nancy asked.

Henry consulted the guest register at the front desk. "Says here, New York City," he told Nancy.

"I wonder what she does for a living," Nancy said.

"I don't know that."

"Do many people come here by themselves?" Nancy asked.

"I'd say that in an average summer we might get two or three people who are here by themselves." Henry ran his large hand over his balding head and sighed with frustration. "Nancy, have you picked up *any* information at all about who might be causing the trouble?"

Nancy paused. She decided that it was too early to suggest suspects. There was too much she still didn't know. "We've been looking into several possibilities," she said, "but we haven't come to any conclusions."

"I'm sure you need more time," said Henry. "After all, you only arrived yesterday."

"Yes," Nancy said. "But try not to worry, Henry. We'll find out who's responsible for all of these weird happenings."

"I sure hope so, Nancy," he said, gazing off into the distance. "I sure hope so."

"Look who we bumped into!" Bess said. She was lounging beside the pool, her face, arms, and legs slathered with oil. Steve Matheson sat next to her wearing his sunglasses, a pair of jeans, and a muscle T-shirt.

"Hi, Nancy," Steve greeted her with a friendly smile. "Ready for a swim?"

"I sure am," she said, tossing her towel into an empty chair next to Bess. She had stopped at the cottage and changed into her swimsuit. "You taking some time off?"

He grinned. "Well, technically I'm on duty. One of my most important jobs is to see that the guests are having a good time. So I come up here occasionally to do just that."

"Well, we're having a great time!" Bess assured him. "Oh, the sun feels so good today!" She settled back in the lounger and closed her eyes.

George swam to the side of the pool and rested her arms along the edge. "Jump in, Nancy," she said. "The water feels great!"

"In a few minutes," Nancy said. She turned to Steve. "Did you hear that another family checked out early this afternoon?"

Steve frowned. "Yeah, Henry told me. I guess

that hanging dummy really scared the little kids."

"But it's not just that," Nancy said. "There've been a lot of strange things going on around here."

"I know," Steve admitted. "It's really a shame. Henry and Ruth are such nice people. And I can't pretend I'm not worried about a job here in the future."

"What do you do during the rest of the year?" Nancy asked.

"I teach high school P.E.," he said. "And coach football."

"Well," Bess said, opening her eyes and sitting up a little, "it would sure make me feel better if I could know without a doubt that *people* were doing these things and not *ghosts!*"

"You don't have to worry about ghosts as long as you stay clear of Horse Island," Steve said. "I don't know why anyone would want to go to the island, anyway. The place gives me the creeps."

"You go there?" Nancy asked, surprised.

"Only when I think one of the guests has decided to go 'exploring,'" he said. "As soon as I find the wayward guest, I tell him to get out, and then I leave as quickly as possible."

Bess leaned forward. "What's it like on the island, Steve?"

Steve sighed. "I don't know that I've seen ghosts, Bess, but I've felt a presence of some kind—something evil—on the island. I don't like the place. Too many bad things have happened there."

"It's amazing what your imagination can do when you're a little nervous in the first place," George commented from the pool.

"Well, whether it's ghosts or hunters, the island isn't a safe place for anybody," Steve said.

Bess shivered. "Don't worry," she said, "you won't catch *me* there!"

Steve glanced back and forth between Nancy and George. "I hope I won't catch any of the guests there."

"George, that water looks so good, I can't wait any longer!" Nancy called out, choosing to ignore Steve's comment.

"Come on in!" George said, grinning.

"Ready for a dip in the pool?" Nancy asked Steve and Bess.

"I'll pass," said Steve.

"Count me out, too," said Bess. "I'm happy just relaxing."

Nancy dived into the pool. She and George swam laps for the next few minutes. When they had finished and had swum back to the edge of the pool, Steve Matheson was gone.

"He had to get back to work," Bess explained. "Nancy, I noticed you didn't promise to stay away from Horse Island."

"That's because I can't," Nancy told her. She hopped up on the edge of the pool, then walked over to the towel she'd left on the chair next to Bess.

"What do you mean?" Bess asked, her voice rising in alarm.

"I'm curious about that island," Nancy said. "And I have to wonder if the stories of ghosts and hunters have anything to do with all the strange things going on at the resort. I'm going to the island, no matter what Steve Matheson has to say."

6

A Visit to Horse Island

"I can't believe we're doing this!" said Bess. "Steve has told us repeatedly *not* to go to Horse Island. And here we are, taking an afternoon trip there! Nancy, it just isn't safe!"

The girls had checked out a canoe at the boat house and were paddling away from shore. Bess was sitting on the bottom of the canoe between Nancy and George, who were paddling.

"I told you, you didn't have to come," Nancy said to Bess over her shoulder.

"What? And let you go all alone? Forget it!" Bess replied. "We couldn't do that, could we, George?"

"Nope," George replied from the stern of the canoe. Although she wasn't as outwardly nervous as Bess, her face wore a tense expression.

"Well," Bess said, looking at the sky, "as if this whole trip weren't dangerous enough already, now it's getting cloudy. Say, what would you guys think about coming back on a bright, sunny day?"

"I'd think you were looking for excuses not to go," Nancy said, grinning.

"And you'd be right," Bess replied seriously.

Nancy smiled at Bess. "It'll be okay, Bess. We'll be back by late afternoon. I just want to see a little of the island."

Bess was plainly not reassured, but she sat in silence as the girls' paddling brought them closer to the island.

"George," Nancy said, "what were those books I saw you pack in your knapsack?"

"Field guides to birds and plant life in this part of the country," George said. "I thought I'd look for wildlife."

"I just hope it isn't *too* wild," Bess mumbled.

It took half an hour more before the girls reached the island. They pulled the canoe up on the beach and looked around.

"It's really pretty here," Nancy observed. "Too bad it isn't available to the guests at the resort."

The island was filled with scrub pines and tall trees. Open areas lined the beach and fingered into the woods.

"How far do you think it is across the island?" asked George.

"Maybe a mile," Nancy guessed. "Come on. We'll leave the canoe here. Let's see what the island has to offer."

Each of the girls had brought a knapsack and a life jacket. They left the bright orange jackets in the canoe and hauled out the knapsacks.

"It looks more and more like rain," Bess said, gazing up at the sky.

"You're right, it does," Nancy agreed. "So let's look around while we have the chance."

"Which direction?" George asked.

"Let's cross the island," Nancy suggested. "That way we'll see two beaches, plus the interior."

"Okay," George said. She pulled the bird and plant books out of her pack and began leafing through them. "It says here that the bluebird is the state bird. We should see some game birds here, too, such as ducks, turkeys, and geese. Also partridges and pheasants."

"Where could the old house be?" Nancy wondered aloud as they began their hike.

The girls soon entered a wooded area that was scattered with occasional patches of open glades, where the rocky ground prevented trees from growing.

"Oh, look," George cried, approaching some wildflowers blowing in the wind. "Black-eyed Susans. I know those without my book." She opened her plant book. "But I don't know these bushes here with the berries." She leafed through the book and stopped at a page. "Oh, they're mountain laurel," she said. "It says here that the berries are poisonous."

Nancy suddenly grabbed George's arm. "Look, George," she said. "There—through the trees. It's the old house!"

Bess gasped. "It's just like a house out of a horror movie!" she said. "A huge Victorian mansion! And the dark clouds overhead sure add to the atmosphere."

George whistled. "That's quite a summer home."

"The financier and his wife must have been very wealthy to afford a place like that," said Nancy.

"That place just *looks* haunted," Bess said. "But I'm glad we don't have to get any closer."

"I have to get a picture of this," Nancy said,

taking her camera from its case. Stepping onto a large rock, Nancy snapped several pictures of the old house.

"Oh, Nancy, let's keep walking," George urged. "I'd love to see it up close!"

Nancy smiled. "So would I. Bess, you can stay here if you want to. We won't take much time."

Bess shivered. "Oh, great! I have the choice of staying here alone or going up to the house with you two?" She thought a moment. "I guess I'll stay here. But don't be long, okay?"

Nancy and George promised they'd be back soon and headed off toward the house.

In ten minutes the girls were standing before the looming Victorian structure. Now faded and flaking, green and white paint had once highlighted the ornamental trim. There was a porch that wrapped around the front of the house. Ornately carved narrow pillars supported the porch roof, which cast the front door deep in shadow. The tallest point of the house was a tower that stood over the two main wings.

"Just look at that tower!" George said. "Wouldn't you love to have a bedroom in that third-floor tower room?"

"I sure would," Nancy agreed. She snapped a few more pictures. "The architecture is incredible. Let's see what the back of the house looks like."

The girls tromped around the side of the house, where thorny brambles scratched their legs. Vines hung from trees that grew close to the house, blocking their path. Finally they found the back door.

"It's boarded up," George pointed out.

Nancy approached the door and rested a hand on the boards. "Wouldn't this house have stories to tell?" she said. As she spoke the board under her hand slid slightly to the side. "What's this?" She moved the board farther, and it fell back from the door.

"That's odd," Nancy said. "This board has been placed on two nailed slats, but it's not actually nailed shut. See? The doorknob is right here. It was covered by that loose board."

"You think someone is going in and out of the house?" George asked.

"It looks that way," Nancy said, jiggling the doorknob. As Nancy suspected, the door behind the boards wasn't locked. With a loud creak, the door swung open into the house. "I'd love to go inside. Maybe we'd learn something about what's going on around here. It would be easy to slip right through the space left by this loose board."

"But, Bess—" George started to say.

"I know," Nancy said. "We can't go now. But I'm definitely coming back later."

After Nancy took a few pictures of the boarded-up door, they walked back to where Bess was waiting for them.

"Oh, good, you're back!" Bess cried with relief. "What was it like up close?"

"No ghosts, but we did discover something interesting," Nancy said. She told Bess about the back door that had been boarded over in such a way as to allow someone to enter.

"That's strange," said Bess. "I wonder who is using the house. And why they'd *want* to. This island gives me the creeps!"

"Well, let's cross the island," Nancy said, gazing up at the dark sky. "I'd like to see some more before it begins to rain."

The girls headed through the woods and out into a clearing in the middle of the island.

"Look at this!" Nancy shouted.

The girls were approaching a fence built with wooden posts and wire.

"This is practically new wood," Nancy observed, kneeling to examine the fence. "Why would someone build a fence here in the middle of the island?"

"It doesn't make sense," George agreed, running her hand along the wooden post. "What's here to fence out? Or fence in?"

"Good question," Nancy said. "I have no idea." She took out her camera again and clicked off a few shots.

"What do you think is going on here?" George asked.

"I don't know," Nancy admitted. "Maybe it's the hunters. But why would they build a fence?"

At that moment a raindrop hit Nancy's nose. Within a few seconds drops of water plopped all around them, making soft splatters on the greenery.

"Let's go," Nancy said, "before we get drenched. I'll come back later." The girls retraced their steps across the island as the rain fell with more and more intensity.

"I'm soaked!" complained Bess, pulling at her wet, sticky blouse. "I'll be glad to get back to the cottage so I can take a long, hot shower."

"I get the shower second," George said.

"You two deserve it," Nancy said. "Thanks for coming along with me to this island. I know neither of you really wanted to come."

"That's okay," Bess said, stepping over a clump of tall weeds and pushing branches out of her way. "I'm just glad we're heading back."

"Me, too, if you want to know the truth," said George. "The house didn't bother me, but these wet clothes feel pretty uncomfortable."

The wind howled, and the girls hunched forward against the downpour.

"It's almost as if the wind wants us back at the house," George shouted at her friends.

"Maybe ghosts can cause storms like this," Bess hollered. "That's why people only see ghosts on dark and stormy nights."

George grinned. "Not likely," she yelled. "It's more probable that people get to imagining things on dark and stormy nights. Right, Nancy?"

"Right," Nancy said, grinning and squinting into the rain that pelted her face.

The wind died down as fast as it had come up, but the rain continued relentlessly.

"How far back to the canoe?" Bess asked.

"It can't be much farther," Nancy said. "I can see the shoreline through the trees."

"Do you think we'll have trouble paddling back in the rain?" George asked Nancy.

"I don't think the rain will be a problem," Nancy said. "If the wind stays low for a while, we shouldn't have trouble And I don't see any lightning."

"Here we are," George said as they came out of

a wooded area and onto the beach. "I remember that fallen birch at the edge of the water. This is the spot where we left the canoe."

The girls stopped dead in their tracks and looked up and down the shore.

Bess was the first to speak. "Nancy!" she said, her eyes filled with horror. "The canoe! *It's gone!*"

7

A Temporary Residence

"What could have happened to the canoe?" Bess gasped.

"Maybe the storm carried it away," George guessed.

"I suppose it's possible," Nancy said as they came closer to the point in the sand where the canoe had been left. She doubted that was what had happened, though. She and George had pulled the canoe up onto the sand so that it was almost completely out of the water.

"Look!" Nancy said. "There are tracks in the sand here where the canoe was." She pointed to where the canoe had been scraped along the sand a few feet. "It was picked up here," she said, pointing to where the tracks stopped, "and carried off." Several footprints in the sand disappeared into the grass.

George turned to face Nancy. "What do we do next?" she asked.

"I think we should find shelter and wait out the storm," Nancy said.

"The house," George said. "Let's go back to the old house."

"No, thanks," Bess said. "I think I'd rather wait right here. Maybe someone will come by in a boat, and I'll flag them down."

"Nobody will be out in a boat in weather like this," Nancy said. She hooked a soaking lock of hair behind one ear. "Let's go back to the house and wait until the rain stops."

"What if that isn't until tomorrow?" Bess asked fearfully. "We'll have to spend the night in that house!"

"We'll all be there together," George said. "At least we won't be out in the cold rain."

"Come on, Bess," Nancy said gently. "We really don't have a choice. George is right. We can't stay out here. It's too wet and cold."

Bess sighed heavily. "I guess you're right," she said. She laughed ruefully. "I can't believe I'm *agreeing* that staying in a haunted house overnight is the better choice!"

Nancy grinned. "It'll be an experience you can share with your grandchildren."

Bess grimaced. "If I live that long."

The girls began their hike back to the old house. After a while they sighted the tower stretched up into the gray and black sky.

When they reached the back door, Nancy moved the loose board and pushed the heavy wooden door open.

"After you," Bess said to Nancy.

Nancy crawled into the house through the space left by the board. George and Bess followed, shutting the door behind them.

"The kitchen," Nancy stated, looking around her.

The room was deep in shadow, but they were able to make out some features. They were in a spacious, old-fashioned kitchen with large wooden cupboards along two of the walls and open spaces where the sink and stove would have been.

"This was obviously updated in the forties or fifties," Nancy said. "This linoleum was very popular back when our parents were growing up. My grandmother's kitchen looked a little like this."

"It's getting so dark," George said. "I wish there was a lantern around here."

"We don't need one," Nancy said with a little

71

smile. She dug into her knapsack and brought out a flashlight.

"I should've known that Nancy would come prepared," George said, grinning.

Nancy snapped on the light. "Let's explore," she said.

"Great!" George said.

"Just don't go anywhere without me," Bess said anxiously.

George and Bess followed Nancy out of the kitchen and into a large paneled room. From the ceiling hung a huge crystal chandelier covered with dust and cobwebs.

"How gorgeous!" Bess said. "This must be the dining room."

"I'll bet the owners entertained a lot of their New York friends right here in this room," Nancy said.

"Maybe just before they drowned in the lake," George said.

"Don't talk about that!" Bess wailed. "I don't even want to think about it."

A howl came from outside that startled Bess.

"Just the wind," said George. "It's started to blow hard again."

The howl came again, and the house shuddered in the shrill wind. They could hear the rain against the windows and trees branches being knocked against the house.

"Let's see the rest of the house," Nancy suggested.

The girls followed Nancy through the dining room and into a room that was even larger. Nancy shone her flashlight on a few large pieces of furniture, which were covered with white sheets.

"This must be the parlor," Nancy said. "They probably received guests here."

"I can't believe the furniture is still here," George said. "Oh, look at this old clock!"

Nancy pointed the flashlight toward the antique timepiece on top of a fireplace mantel.

"It's ticking!" George gasped.

"What? That can't be!" Nancy said, moving swiftly to join George. Bess followed close behind.

"It *is* working!" Nancy exclaimed. She checked her watch. "And the time is correct." She put her hands on her hips and turned out toward the room. "Well, I guess we were right."

"What?" asked Bess.

"Someone does come here," Nancy said.

"Who could it be?" Bess asked.

"I wish I knew," Nancy said. "Probably the

same person who built the fence in the middle of the island and fixed the boarded-up door. I'm wondering if this person could have any connection with the weird things going on at the resort."

The girls passed into the large front foyer of the house. It, too, was paneled with dark wood. Nancy looked carefully at the front door, which was nailed shut.

"This door has not been rigged so that it could open," Nancy observed. "That person apparently decided to use the back door for his—or her—comings and goings."

They continued their tour of the house and found a library on the ground floor that still held rows of hardcover books, now damp and mildewed in the humid lake air. A grand piano stood in one corner of the room. Nancy moved the piano bench out of the way, blew some dust off the keys, and played a few chords.

"It's horribly out of tune," she said. "At least we know that the person who set up housekeeping here isn't a pianist. No self-respecting musician would play on an instrument that sounds as bad as this."

The girls moved back into the foyer. The sun, invisible behind the thick layers of clouds, was setting, and what little natural light they had had from outside was diminishing.

"Want to see what's upstairs?" Nancy asked.

"Not really," Bess said. "But I have a feeling that you two want to explore some more."

"Do you want to wait here?" George asked.

"And be down here all alone?" Bess said. "Forget it! I'm coming with you!"

A grand staircase stretched in front of them up into the shadows of the second floor. Nancy let Bess and George start up first so she could shine the light on the steps as they climbed.

"Don't depend on this railing," Nancy said, wiggling the banister. "It's falling apart."

The girls made their way slowly up the stairs, the steps creaking from their weight. At the top they found a long hallway with rooms on either side. The doors to all the rooms were shut.

Nancy opened the first door on the left, and the girls peeked inside.

"Completely empty," George whispered. "Let's try another room."

They crossed the hall and opened the door. "Another empty room," Bess said.

They walked into the room, and Nancy stepped to the far window. "It's completely dark now," Nancy said, "but the rain's stopped."

75

George and Bess joined her at the window. "I think I see a hint of light on the horizon," George said. "Maybe it'll be sunny tomorrow."

Bess gasped. "Did you see that?"

"What?" George asked, looking out the window.

"A light. I saw a light down in the trees!" Bess said excitedly. "There it is again! Did you see it?"

"I didn't see anything. Did you, Nancy?" asked George.

"No," Nancy said quietly. "Who would be roaming out there on a night like this? Maybe it was your imagination, Bess." Nancy couldn't help but worry, though. Could the person who had taken their canoe still be out there? "Maybe we should block off that entrance to the kitchen, just in case," she said, trying to keep her voice casual.

"Good idea," George agreed.

The girls hurried down to the dark kitchen. Sweeping the room with the beam of her flashlight, Nancy looked for something to prop against the door. "Hey, maybe we're in luck," she said as her beam landed on the windowsill. There sat a long, rusty skeleton key.

Nancy put the key in the keyhole. "It locks from the inside," she said, pulling at the door. "No one's getting in now. Come on," Nancy said.

"Let's go back to exploring the rooms." They climbed the stairs once again and continued their tour of the second floor. In some of the rooms, old bed frames and large wooden wardrobes still stood.

"How do you think we could get to the tower?" George asked as they headed back to the staircase. "I'd love to see what's up there."

"I'll bet the stairs are inside one of those front rooms," Nancy figured. "Let's look." They went back to the first room they'd explored and entered. Nancy spotted a door with the beam of her flashlight.

A large iron key, like the one she'd used in the kitchen, sat in the door's keyhole. Nancy crossed the room and pulled open the unlocked door. "Bingo! A staircase," she said.

George and Bess followed as Nancy began to climb the steep, narrow stairs. A flapping noise from overhead startled them.

"*Bats!*" Bess shrieked. *"Let's get out of here!"*

The three girls moved quickly back down the stairs and slammed the door behind them.

"Oh, I *hate* bats!" Bess said, shuddering. "Let's get downstairs."

Nancy and George didn't argue, and they all hurried out of the room and down the steps to the ground floor.

"We'd better find a comfortable place to spend the night," Nancy said. "Let's try the parlor."

The girls moved into the parlor and threw off the sheets that covered the furniture. Two long couches would sleep two of the girls, they decided. The third would have to sleep sitting up in one of the large overstuffed chairs.

"We'll take turns," Nancy suggested.

"I'll take the chair first," Bess said. "I couldn't go to sleep now, anyway!"

The girls agreed that Bess would awaken Nancy first, and they would trade sleeping places. Nancy and George lay down on the couches, and Bess settled into the big chair.

It was quiet in the house except for the soft ticking of the clock on the mantel and the howl of the wind outside. Bess sat in the chair, her eyes darting around the room.

Nancy curled up on the couch and pulled one of the sheets over her. She soon fell into a light sleep. In her dreams she was climbing the stairs to the tower, bats swooping at her head. As she raised her arms to fend them off, a light appeared behind the bats. Then she saw the ghostly figure of a person—but she couldn't see who it was. The light grew nearer, and she thought the person was coming toward her. Nancy tried to scream, but her voice was frozen with terror. If only she could see who it was.

Nancy's eyes snapped open. At first she was disoriented. Then she remembered where she was. Relieved that the horrifying apparition had been nothing more than a bad dream, Nancy sat up.

Rubbing her eyes, she looked around the dark room. Someone *was* shining a light on her, but Nancy was blinded by it and couldn't see who was behind it. She looked away from the light and saw that the chair that Bess had been in was empty.

Nancy's heart thumped with alarm. Then she saw someone standing in front of the window, pointing the flashlight out into the night.

Suddenly Bess staggered back from the window and let out a piercing scream.

8

The Island's Inhabitants

"Hurry!" Bess shrieked. "Come see the ghost!"

Nancy raced to the window.

"Where is it?" Nancy asked Bess, who was trembling from head to foot.

"Where?" George demanded, joining them. "I don't see anything!"

Bess expelled a lungful of air. "It's gone!" she whispered. "It dissolved into thin air. Didn't you see it?"

"I'm afraid not," Nancy said.

"Neither did I," said George.

"Oh, Nancy, we've got to get off this island!" Bess said. "I *know* there's a ghost out there! He *wanted* me to see him!"

"We will get off the island," Nancy assured her. "We will, but we have to wait until morning."

George and Nancy persuaded Bess to rest on the couch.

"I'll take the chair," Nancy said.

The night seemed endless, but finally, after many wakeful hours, the three girls fell asleep. When they awoke, the morning sun was streaming through the windows, slanting across the wooden floor in the parlor.

"Oh, I wish I had a toothbrush," George grumbled as she perched on the edge of the couch, stretching her arms overhead and yawning.

"I'd settle for some tooth*paste*," Nancy said, sitting up in the chair. "And a little fresh water."

"I could go for some fried eggs and hash browns," Bess said. "And a glass of orange juice and a cup of hot coffee."

"Oh, don't talk about food," George groaned, waving at Bess. "I'm starved." She glanced at the clock on the mantel. "It's already nine in the morning."

"Let's get our stuff together and walk back to the beach," Nancy said. "Maybe someone will come by in a boat, and we can flag them over to pick us up."

"Good idea," Bess said, more anxious than any of them to get off the island. "Even though the sun is up and the house looks less scary, I still believe absolutely that I saw a ghost last night! It was the ghost of the financier, I'm positive!"

"What about the financier's wife?" Nancy asked, winking at George. "I mean, did you see a man rather than a woman?"

Bess thought for a moment. "Well, I guess I can't be absolutely sure," she said. "I saw a figure with fog and mist all around it, and it was looking right at me! Then, when you and George came to see it, it vanished! I *know* it wants us off the island!"

"Well, we will oblige as soon as we can find a way," Nancy said. "Come on. Let's start walking."

The girls picked up their knapsacks and headed out the back door, arranging the loose board on the door to look just as they had found it.

"It has really warmed up," Nancy said, gazing at the blue sky above them.

"Yeah," George said. "It sure is good to be out of that dark, damp house and into the warm, fresh air!"

"Before we go," Nancy said, "I want to check the exact spot where Bess saw the—uh—"

"The ghost," Bess prompted.

"Whatever it was that she saw," Nancy said with a little smile at Bess. "Show us the spot, Bess."

Bess walked around the side of the house and pointed to a spot directly across from the window at which she'd been standing the night before.

"There," she said, pointing across the clearing toward the edge of the woods. "It was standing right there."

Nancy walked directly to the spot. "Here?" she said.

"Yes," Bess confirmed, standing back a little.

George joined Nancy. "Let's start on the ground," Nancy said. "Look for footprints, anything that could have been left behind."

The girls bent over and began their search.

"This is a waste of time," Bess called out. "A ghost wouldn't drop a comb. What use would a ghost have for a comb? And it wouldn't leave a lapel pin. Who ever heard of a ghost wearing jewelry?"

"How about a pair of sunglasses?" Nancy asked her.

"A ghost doesn't go out in the sun," Bess pointed out. "And it wouldn't worry about wrinkles around its eyes, anyway." George laughed at Bess.

"Well, *this* ghost is apparently concerned about sun glare," Nancy said, holding up a pair of dark glasses.

"*What?*" Bess gasped. "Let me see those!" She hurried over to Nancy and took the glasses.

"Of course, we don't know for sure when these were dropped here," Nancy said. "Last night certainly wouldn't have been a time for *anyone* to wear sunglasses."

"That's right," George said. "Maybe someone exploring the island a day or so ago could have dropped them."

"Or the person who keeps the clock running accurately inside the house," Nancy said, tucking the sunglasses into her knapsack.

The girls started their walk toward the beach. They moved through the heavily wooded area and then into a clearing.

"Oh, look," Bess said, approaching a small plant. "Here are some berries. I think I'll start on my breakfast right here."

"No!" George said, grabbing Bess's arm. "That's the mountain laurel bush I saw yesterday. The berries are poisonous, remember?"

"Oh, George, you're right!" Bess gasped, alarmed by the close call.

Nancy cocked her head and looked around her. "Do you hear something?" she asked.

George and Bess listened.

"I do hear something," Bess said. "It sounds like thunder. But it can't be—there isn't a cloud in the sky."

"I hear it, too," said George. The thundering sound was growing louder by the moment.

"It's coming from that direction," Nancy said, pointing to a stretch of clear land that, like a hallway, separated the woods into two sections. The sound kept growing louder and louder until it became an almost deafening rumble.

"Oh, no!" gasped Bess. An amazing sight had suddenly appeared from around a bend in the clearing.

"Horses!" yelled George above the noise.

"Get out of the way!" Nancy screamed at her friends.

Galloping at them was a herd of wild, stampeding horses!

9

Rescued

The three girls took off running as fast as they could through the open area, across the path of the wildly running horses. The girls headed for the nearest group of trees they could find.

"We'll never make it!" screamed Bess.

"Run for the trees!" yelled Nancy, taking Bess's arm and pulling her along.

The girls entered the woods just as the herd of horses pounded through the clearing only a few feet away from them. Breathing heavily, the girls turned to watch the herd storm by.

"Man, that was close!" George panted.

"Where did they all come from?" Nancy asked breathlessly.

"Yeah," Bess said, "I thought the wild horses on the island had been captured and tamed years ago."

The girls watched until the last of the horses had galloped past them.

"They *were* beautiful," George said.

"And obviously wild," said Bess.

"This is really strange," Nancy said. "We'll have to ask the Steadmans about the horses." She gazed at her two friends, who were beginning to breathe easier. "Ready to move on?"

"I'm *more* than ready to leave this island," Bess said.

"Me, too," George agreed.

Nancy, Bess, and George headed for the beach.

"Look!" Nancy said, pointing into the woods. "I see someone. Isn't that Teresa Diamond?"

The girls peered into the distance. Teresa was walking through the woods, dressed in jeans and a light blue workshirt.

"Can we trust her?" asked George. "Maybe she's the one who took our canoe."

"I don't know what to do," Nancy admitted. "If she's the culprit, I don't want to walk right up to her. But she may be our only way off the island. Let's follow her for a while and see what she does."

Nancy, Bess, and George followed Teresa, who

was walking away from them. It seemed that Teresa was increasing her pace, and soon the girls had to run through the woods to keep her in sight as she disappeared behind trees and rocks. When they reached the beach, the girls stopped and looked around them.

"Do you see her?" George asked breathlessly.

"No," Nancy said unhappily. "I think we've lost her."

Just then the girls heard a motor revving to life in the distance. "She's in a motorboat!" Nancy cried. "Come on!"

Racing down the length of the beach, they came to a cove just in time to see Teresa Diamond pulling away.

"Hey, come back!" Bess yelled. The woman looked up at them. It was obvious that she'd heard Bess's cry. She stared at them for a moment, then abruptly turned and continued out onto the lake.

"Well, what's *her* problem?" Bess cried angrily.

"That's what I'd like to know," Nancy said. "Something's going on with that woman, and I'm going to find out what it is!"

"Come on," George said. "Let's go back to the beach where we left our canoe yesterday. Maybe someone will come along."

The girls walked along the beach and settled down in the warm sand.

"It's really warming up," Bess noted. "The sun feels so good." She sighed. "If that Diamond woman had given us a lift, I'd be standing in a warm shower right now, thinking about the jelly doughnut I would have for breakfast at the lodge."

Nancy sat looking out over the lake, wondering if Teresa had anything to do with the disappearance of their canoe. Was it just a coincidence that she happened to show up on this particular morning, when the girls were stranded? And why would she run off instead of helping them?

"I wonder how long till we get rescued," George said.

The girls sat and waited for an hour before Nancy straightened up and called out, "Hey! Look! Canoes!"

The girls jumped to their feet and waved their arms. "Here we are! Over here!" they yelled.

One of the people in a canoe pointed to the girls and waved. The group turned from their course and headed toward the girls on the island.

"Uh-oh," Bess said as they approached. "It's Steve Matheson. He's not going to be happy to see us here."

The group of four canoes stopped just offshore. "What are you doing on the island?" Steve called out angrily, squinting into the sun. Bess had been right. He was furious.

"We wanted to look around, but someone swiped our canoe," Nancy responded. "Can you take on three passengers?"

"Come on," Steve ordered. "I've got room for two in my canoe. A third can ride in this canoe." He pointed to a canoe paddled by a young couple.

The girls waded out into the water. Nancy placed her knapsack and camera in Steve's canoe.

"What were you up to? A little photo expedition?" he asked sarcastically, helping Nancy into the canoe.

"Not exactly," Nancy replied stiffly. George pulled herself up into Steve's canoe, and Bess joined the couple.

Soon they were back at the boat house. Steve hadn't spoken another word all the way back. But as the girls were walking away from the boat house, he ran to catch up with them.

"Sorry if I was rude," he apologized. "It's just that you did a really dangerous and dumb thing by going there. Did you run into hunters?"

"No," said Nancy. She pulled the sunglasses

she'd found out of her bag. "Do you know who these belong to?" she asked.

He took the glasses and examined them. "I know a lot of people who wear sunglasses, but I don't know whose these particular glasses are."

"Do you know of anyone who lives on the island?" Nancy asked. "There were signs that the house is being used by someone."

"You're kidding," Steve said.

"Well, someone has been there recently," Nancy told him as she and the girls turned toward their cabin. "Oh, and Steve, there *are* still horses on the island. They nearly trampled us!"

"What?" Steve cried.

Nancy nodded. "I'll tell you about it later. We need to clean up and get some food. And I want to talk to the Steadmans."

Nancy, Bess, and George headed back to their cottage. After showers and a change of clothes, they walked to the lodge for lunch.

"I'll bet I lost five pounds on Horse Island." Bess said as the girls sat down at a table next to a large window. "So I can afford to stuff myself now. I'm so hungry I could eat an entire meal for a family of six!"

After the waitress had brought their food, Nancy glimpsed Henry Steadman across the room. She waved to him, and he strode over to their table.

"Hi, girls," he said. "I see you're having our famous cheese soup. How is it?"

"Heavenly," Bess sighed. "It really fills in the empty spots. We've eaten very little in the last twenty-four hours."

Henry looked puzzled. "We couldn't entice you to the lodge for a good breakfast?"

"Oh," Nancy said, "the food is wonderful! No, we spent yesterday and last night on Horse Island without a canoe to get us back."

"How did you get out to the island?" Henry asked.

"We checked out a canoe yesterday," Nancy explained. "We beached the canoe for a walk around the island, and when we returned, the canoe was gone!"

"We spent the night in the financier's old mansion," George added.

Henry looked alarmed. "Are you girls all right?"

Nancy nodded. "We're just fine," she reassured him. "But I have some questions to ask you."

"Sure," Henry said. "What do you want to know?"

"We were nearly run over by a herd of stampeding wild horses," Nancy told him. "Are you aware that there are still horses on the island?"

"Sounds like you three had quite an adventure," Henry said. He stroked his chin. "Well, I'm not surprised about the horses. Although I haven't seen them myself, I've heard several local people say that they've seen the horses swimming to and from the island from the valley on the other side of the lake."

"Are you aware that someone has been visiting that island?" Nancy asked.

"No," Henry said. "But what does the island have to do with our resort? Do you think there's a connection?"

"Maybe," Nancy said. "We just don't know yet."

George, who was gazing out the window, reached over and tapped Henry's arm. "Is there a bonfire on the beach today?" she asked.

"No, why?" Henry said.

"Isn't that smoke I see floating out over the lake?" George asked.

The color drained from Henry's face. "Yes, it is! What in the world—"

He got up and rushed out of the dining room with Nancy, Bess, and George close behind.

They raced down the lane, following the smoke. It took only moments to see where the smoke was coming from.

"Oh, no!" Bess screamed. "Nancy, it's our cottage! *It's on fire!*"

10

Unjust Desserts

Smoke billowed out of the cottage windows. Nancy flung the door open and staggered backward from the choking smoke.

"Get away from there, Nancy!" Henry shouted to her.

Staff and guests came running from all directions.

"Get the hose!" Henry yelled to one of his employees. "And buckets!"

Within a minute water was pouring into the girls' cottage from the hose, and a line of staff and several guests—including Nancy, Bess, and George—were passing buckets of water from the lake to use in extinguishing the blaze.

The fire seemed to be isolated in the front room and was quickly drenched. Henry, Nancy, Bess, and George walked into the cottage and stepped over the burned, wet rubble.

The girls searched through the cottage. Most of the damage was not from the fire, but from smoke and water.

"The picnic basket and its contents were destroyed," Nancy reported to Henry. "And so were a few items of clothing and the table-cloth."

"But how did it start?" George asked. "Did an electrical appliance short out?"

Nancy was poking around in the rubble and ash. "Look at this," she said. Henry and the girls moved closer. "This is dry grass and brush. See? Some of it didn't burn completely before we put out the fire. No wonder the fire smoked so heavily."

"How did grass and brush get into the cottage?" Bess asked.

"Someone brought it in," Nancy said. "This fire was set!"

Henry looked at her sharply. "Arson?"

"It sure looks that way," Nancy told him. "The fire was smoky but did very little damage. It seems as if the arsonist wanted the fire to be spotted right away."

"You think the fire was another warning?" George asked.

"I think so," Nancy said.

"Because you're helping me on this case?" Henry asked. Then he shook his head. "Well, that does it. You girls should stop investigating at once. I would never forgive myself if something happened—"

"We're fine, Henry," George said. "We won't do anything dangerous."

"It's already been dangerous for you," Henry said.

"Don't worry about us," Nancy said. "We just need to get to the bottom of this before anything worse happens."

Henry pulled a set of keys out of his pocket. "The family next door just left this morning," he said. "You girls move into that cottage so we can get this place fixed up again."

"Henry," Nancy said, "who else has a set of those keys or could get their hands on a set?"

"There's an extra set in my office," Henry replied, "and the only people who can go in there are staff. Why do you ask?"

"There's no sign of a break-in here," Nancy said. "It looks like someone had a key. We've been careful about locking the door and the screens on the windows."

"I'll have to hide the extra set," Henry said, "until this crooked person is caught. Nancy, I'm so sorry about all you and Bess and George have gone through. Let's hope this ends soon."

Henry left, and Ann and Carrie came over from next door to help the girls move into the empty cottage.

"This place is getting scary," said Carrie after the last of the girls' belongings were carried into the cottage.

"Did either of you happen to see anyone around our cottage before the fire started?" Nancy asked them.

"Well," Ann said thoughtfully, "I was walking home from the stables with Rodney about a half hour before the fire—"

"You were with Rodney?" Carrie interrupted. "You took a long walk with that dream-boat?"

"Go on," Nancy pressed.

"And I saw that strange guest—that woman in cottage fourteen—standing near your bedroom window," Ann said.

"Did you speak to her?" Nancy asked.

"Yes," Ann said, "I said hi, but she just turned around quickly and walked away."

Bess's eyes grew big. "Do you think *she* was responsible?"

"I don't know," Nancy said. "I wonder why she was hanging around here."

"Well, I don't know, either," Carrie said, "but I'd watch that woman if I were you."

The girls thanked Ann and Carrie, said good-bye to them, and proceeded to arrange their belongings in the new cottage.

"The island is the key," Nancy said. "I'm sure of it."

"Why? How do you know that?" George said.

"I think the fire was set to selectively destroy a piece of evidence," Nancy said.

"What evidence?" asked Bess.

"The film," Nancy said. "I put my camera and film of the island in the picnic basket. They were the only things destroyed in the fire!"

"I love it!" Bess exclaimed. "A fish fry with all my favorite foods!" The aroma of steamed clams had her mouth watering.

The girls stood in line with the other guests in the early evening, holding their plates. A long table had been set outside the lodge and was piled high with salads, fresh fruit, corn on the cob, and grilled vegetables. At the end of the table was an open grill where breaded fish was frying.

Otis presided over the grill. He was busy with

his work and didn't look up. Occasionally he would give orders to a kitchen helper, who would scurry off to carry out his commands.

"Otis's assistants seem to respect him," Nancy observed, "but he looks like someone who wouldn't be easy to work for."

The girls picked up their food and seated themselves at one of the many picnic tables that had been set out for the guests. They sat across from Mr. and Mrs. Savage, the older couple they had met the first night at the lodge dining room.

"Have you had any more prowlers?" Nancy asked them, biting into a piece of fried fish.

"We certainly have, last night," Mrs. Savage told Nancy. "This time, along with the tapping on the window in the middle of the night, the prowler played a tape of someone screaming."

Nancy frowned. "You're sure it was a tape?"

"Oh, yes," Mrs. Savage said. "It was just outside the window. We called Henry Steadman, but by the time he arrived, the prowler was gone."

"Are you frightened?" Nancy asked.

The Savages glanced at each other. "We weren't until we heard about the fire in your cottage," Mrs. Savage said. "When that happened we decided to leave several days early. We're going tomorrow."

Mr. Savage nodded his head toward the far end of the table. "Look at how few people are left here," he remarked.

"I would have expected more," Nancy said.

"Three more families left this afternoon after hearing about your fire," Mr. Savage said. "Several new guests who haven't heard about the trouble here have arrived, but many of the others have left."

Nancy sighed. She felt so helpless. She'd been here several days and still was no closer to catching the culprit than she had been on the first day.

"This pie is incredible!" Bess gushed.

"You haven't finished your supper!" George chided her.

"Who cares?" Bess said. "I'm on vacation!" Everyone laughed.

The girls finished their meal and joined a group of young people playing badminton.

"I think I've had enough," Bess said, holding her stomach after several minutes of play.

"But we just started!" George said.

"I have a bad stomachache," Bess said. "I think I'll go back to the cottage and lie down."

"Boy, me, too!" said one of the girls who had been on the horseback ride. "I guess all that food and exercise didn't mix."

When several others complained of stomachaches, Nancy became alarmed. She walked over to the food table and examined the dishes.

"George!" she called out sharply, stopping in front of the blueberry pie that Bess had eaten.

"What?" In a moment George was right beside her.

Nancy pointed to several berries on top of the pie. "Aren't those from a mountain laurel bush?" she asked.

George looked at the berries and then, with a horrified expression, looked at Nancy.

"Yes!" she said. "They're poisonous!"

11

Suspicions

"We'd better check with the closest hospital," Nancy told George. "They may want to send ambulances here."

Not wasting a moment, George ran off to make the call. Nancy looked around for Otis. The crowd had thinned out a little, but there were still more than a dozen guests remaining who were playing badminton and chatting around the picnic tables.

Otis wasn't in sight, and Nancy wondered if he had a reason for leaving the festivities early. Could he have been responsible for the guests' illness? He was certainly in the best position to poison the food. Still, Nancy thought, he had to realize that he would be the most likely suspect if he tampered with the food. But because of his bad temperament and anger toward the Steadmans, he certainly was someone she needed to talk to.

Maybe he had gone back to the kitchen, Nancy thought. She moved quickly down the lane to the lodge dining room and found her way to the kitchen. Three of the helpers Nancy had seen earlier were busy washing dishes. She found the large man sitting at a desk in an office off the kitchen. He seemed to be involved in paperwork.

"Excuse me. Otis?" Nancy said.

The man looked up at her and frowned. "Yes?" he said in a deep baritone voice.

"I'm Nancy Drew, a guest here."

"Guests don't generally barge into the kitchen," he said impatiently. He went back to his work.

"Well," Nancy continued, "I certainly didn't mean to bother you, but I'd like to talk with you for a few minutes."

"Yes?" Otis left the question hanging and didn't look up.

"Are you aware that one of your desserts tonight contained poison berries?" Nancy asked.

Otis looked up sharply. "What are you saying?" he asked angrily. He rose from the desk and took a step toward Nancy.

Nancy held her ground. "My friends and I were hiking yesterday and found a mountain laurel bush covered with berries," she said. "A field guide to plants in this area says they're poisonous. My friend and a few others ate the dessert, not recognizing the berries, and now they're complaining of stomachaches."

"I don't know what you're talking about!" Otis thundered, his face red with anger. "That's preposterous! The very thought that I'd put inedible berries in my desserts!"

"Where do you get your berries?" Nancy asked.

"At the fruit wholesaler in town!" Otis shouted, still furious.

Nancy gazed a moment at Otis. He sure was displaying his bad temper for her in a grand style.

"Do you still have the leftover food?" Nancy asked, unblinking.

Otis stalked into the kitchen furiously. "Yes!" he barked, and he led Nancy to a table piled with the pots and dishes with bits of food still in them. He pointed to them and took a step backward. "Maybe this will straighten you out."

Nancy stepped up to the table and looked over

the array of plates. "Here," she said. "This is the dessert." There was half a pie remaining on the tray.

Otis looked at the pan and gasped. "This is *not* my pie!" he bellowed. "I did not make this dessert!"

"Maybe you can tell me," Nancy said. "Does this serving dish belong to the resort?"

"Yes," Otis admitted. "It does. I was looking for it yesterday when I was getting organized for the fish fry. I never found it. *Someone stole it from me!*"

"That is certainly possible," Nancy said.

"Possible?" Otis repeated. "That's exactly what happened!" He looked at her suspiciously. "Perhaps *you* took it and set me up!"

"I assure you," Nancy said evenly, "that is not what happened. I think this is likely to have been arranged by the person who has pulled a number of other tricks around here. Did you see anyone hanging around during the preparation of the cookout?"

"No," Otis said. "But when I get my hands on him—"

"We'll turn him—or her—over to the police," Nancy said. "But tell me, Otis—I understand that you have had some arguments with the Steadmans about your salary. Would you—"

"How *dare* you accuse me of this terrible act!" Otis raged.

"You just accused me," Nancy reminded him.

"I am having an ongoing discussion with Henry Steadman about what he should pay me," Otis said. "I'm an *artist*. And now that people are leaving this resort in *droves* because of several unfortunate incidents, Steadman has reduced the size of my staff! It's getting harder and harder to make a living in this place."

"Well, if you will excuse me, I think I'd better go and talk with Henry Steadman," Nancy said. "He should be told that he may have a serious situation on his hands."

Nancy turned and walked out the kitchen door just as George came hurrying up the lane.

"It's okay," George said, smiling with relief. "Bess and the others will be all right, probably by tomorrow. The doctor I talked to said that the mountain laurel berries will cause discomfort but nothing worse. I just checked on Bess. She's asleep now."

"Oh, good!" Nancy said, and she expelled a lungful of air. "Come on, George. Henry should know about this last episode."

Nancy and George walked around to the front of the lodge and inside the main door. They found Henry and Ruth behind the desk.

107

"Hi," Nancy greeted them both. "May we talk to you?"

"Sure," Henry said, frowning. "You girls look serious. I hope nothing more has happened."

"I'm afraid something has," Nancy said. She and George told the Steadmans about the poisonous berries in the dessert. "Fortunately, everyone will be fine after an uncomfortable night," Nancy said. "I just talked with Otis," she continued. "He was furious that I would question him about it."

"That sounds just like Otis!" Ruth said angrily.

"Now, Ruth," Henry said. He gazed at the girls. "Ruth thinks Otis is a—well, a—"

"A madman!" she said.

"Madman?" Nancy questioned.

"Oh, it's his artistic temperament," Henry explained. "He flies off the handle all the time, but he wouldn't hurt anybody."

"I wouldn't be so sure about that!" Ruth said. "He threatened you last year, remember? He said if he didn't get a substantial raise, you would be sorry!"

Henry turned to Nancy. "Otis is here because he wants to live in the country. But he thinks he should be earning big-city money. We simply can't afford to pay him more than we do now.

He's worth every penny we do pay him—the food here is a big reason people keep coming back. But we just can't give him more."

"Do you think Otis could be responsible for the weird things going on here?" George asked.

"Yes!" Ruth said.

"No," Henry said at the same time.

Nancy smiled a little. "Well, we'll keep him in mind, anyway."

"Can I join this powwow?" a voice called out.

The girls looked up to see Steve Matheson approaching them. He was wearing a pair of jeans and an old blue-and-white cotton shirt that had a tear in the sleeve. "Sure," Nancy said.

"Say, Henry," Steve said, "I went over to Horse Island, just as you asked me to. I didn't see any horses." He looked at Nancy. "You girls really saw wild horses?"

"We sure did!" Nancy said. "They nearly trampled us, but we managed to get out of the way just in time."

"That's incredible!" he said. "I thought they'd been captured years ago."

"Oh, every season we hear of someone who has seen the horses swimming out to the island," Henry said. "It would be exciting to see them. Of course, if they *are* there, they're protected by law."

"Henry," Steve said, "I'm going to make a quick run into town for supplies."

"Sure thing," Henry said. He excused himself to make a call to the hospital about the berries. Steve left, and Nancy and George said goodbye to Ruth.

"Let's pay a visit to Teresa Diamond," Nancy said to George. "I want to ask her why she was on the island this morning."

When the girls knocked on Teresa's door, it was yanked open immediately. Teresa was wearing a pair of jeans, a cotton blouse, and a red bandanna around her neck. She did not look happy to see Nancy.

"Teresa," Nancy said, "we were stranded on Horse Island last night. This morning we saw you on the island. We called to you for help, but you ran away, jumped into a motorboat, and sped off."

"What are you talking about?" Teresa said angrily. "I wasn't on the island. I was here working all morning."

"We saw you," George said. "There was no mistake. It was you."

"What sort of work do you do?" Nancy asked.

"I'm a writer," she said. "Now, unless you have any other questions"—she glanced back and forth between Nancy and George—"I have

110

to get back to work." Before Nancy or George had a chance to respond, she slammed the door in their faces.

"I think I'll take a little walk," Nancy said to George later that evening. "To think about the case."

"Sure," George said. "Bess is still sound asleep, and I'm going to start that new novel I brought."

"See you later," Nancy said. She stepped out of the cottage and closed the door softly behind her.

The night was cool, and Nancy zipped her jacket. The air smelled of the surrounding pine trees. The lake lapped gently against the dock not more than two hundred feet away. Nancy took a deep breath of the night air and started off.

She really didn't have a destination in mind, just a quiet place to walk and think. She looked up the hill and decided to head to the swimming pool.

This case is certainly a tough one, Nancy thought. So many strange things are going on, but nothing really points to any one suspect. Still, it was definitely noteworthy that Otis held such hostile feelings toward the Steadmans. He certainly believed he had good cause. And Teresa

Diamond was hiding something, and she apparently had an interest in the island. But why?

Nancy reached the top of the hill, opened a gate, and walked along the sidewalk that circled the heated pool. A sign saying that the pool closed at ten P.M. was dimly lit by the light near the gate. The lights surrounding the pool were turned off, and no one was around. Nancy strolled to the edge of the pool, sat down, kicked off her sandals, and dipped her feet in the water.

A soft noise from behind startled her. Nancy turned but saw nothing. Just an animal, she decided, turning back to the water.

Suddenly, from out of the darkness, someone grabbed Nancy from behind. Before she could react, Nancy was pushed into the pool. A strong pair of hands forced her head underwater as she held her breath and thrashed her arms and legs desperately to free herself!

12

Follow That Car!

Her lungs nearly bursting, Nancy dug her finger-nails into the hands of her attacker. She couldn't budge from their grasp. She opened her eyes and saw only the black water.

Knowing that she couldn't hold her breath a moment longer, Nancy managed to get one of the hands to her mouth. She bit down hard, and her assailant immediately released her.

Shooting above the water's surface, Nancy threw her head back out of the water and gulped in great gasps of air. She grasped the edge of the pool with both hands and stayed there a moment, breathing heavily.

She suddenly realized that her attacker could

be standing over her. She looked around, but no one was there. Her assailant had apparently disappeared into the darkness.

Nancy heaved herself out of the pool with the small amount of strength she had left and walked to the electrical box on a pole at the far side of the pool. She flipped a switch, and instantly the pool area was illuminated with bright overhead lights.

She was alone at the pool now, she was sure of it. There was no place for her attacker to hide in the immediate vicinity. Her eyes swept over the deck, and something red caught her attention.

She walked over to it. It was a red bandanna, lying at the spot next to the pool where she'd been attacked.

A red bandanna, Nancy thought, just like the one Teresa had been wearing earlier in the evening!

"You really think it was Teresa who tried to drown you?" Bess asked in a low voice.

The girls had gotten up early to stake out Teresa's cottage. Bess was feeling weak, but she insisted on joining her friends. They were sitting at a picnic table behind a bush where they had a clear view of the cottage. They would be able to see—without being seen—if Teresa left.

"Her scarf doesn't *prove* that she was responsible," Nancy said, "but it makes her the likely suspect."

"She sure is big enough to overpower you," Bess said.

"Obviously she didn't mean to drown me," said Nancy. "It was another warning—just like all the rest of the warnings at the resort."

"And a pretty serious warning," George said, looking worried. "They seem to be getting worse and worse. Have you noticed?"

"You're right," Nancy agreed. "They started out with a harmless snake in a tackle box, but now this creep is using fire, poisoning, and a near-drowning to scare everyone." Nancy set her mouth in a tight line. "We've got to find out what is going on before anyone is seriously injured—or worse!"

Suddenly George grabbed Nancy's arm and put a finger to her lips. She pointed at Teresa's cottage, where a door had just opened. The girls watched Teresa lock the door behind her and then go to her car, which was parked on the far side of the cottage.

Nancy gestured for Bess and George to move away. "Our car," she whispered, and they took off toward the side of their cottage, where Nancy had parked.

"I don't want Teresa to see us," Nancy said as

they seated themselves in the car, "so I'll stay a little behind her."

They followed Teresa down the lane and out of the resort. Teresa drove into the thick woods and kept the car moving at a steady but slow speed to avoid the bumps in the road.

"I wonder where she's going," George said.

"Well," Nancy said, "she told me yesterday that she was working—and she's a writer. Maybe this is a working vacation."

Nancy slowed down a little more when Teresa got to the highway.

"She's heading toward town," Nancy said.

"Maybe she needs supplies of some sort," said George.

"Or maybe she's meeting somebody," Nancy guessed.

They followed far behind for the ten miles into town. Teresa pulled up at a public telephone booth on the sidewalk along the main road and got out. Nancy stopped the car a half block away. Teresa walked into the booth and picked up the phone.

"Now, why would she do that?" Bess wondered. "The cottages have telephones."

"Yes," Nancy said, "but they're linked to the switchboard in the lodge office. Maybe this is a very private phone call."

"It's long distance, anyway," said George. She had pulled a pair of binoculars out of her backpack and was studying Teresa through the glasses. "She pulled a telephone credit card out of her bag. See? She's dialing and referring to the card."

"Interesting," Nancy said.

Teresa finished her call in about three minutes and hung up. She got into her car and pulled out onto the main street.

"Are we going to follow her?" Bess asked.

"Definitely," Nancy said. She pulled the silver car out onto the street and, once again, trailed behind Teresa.

At the next corner, Teresa turned right, and Nancy followed. At the corner after that, Teresa turned left and sped up.

"Uh-oh," Nancy said. "She knows she's being followed." Nancy sped up, too, and kept close behind her.

Suddenly Teresa pulled into a parking lot.

"We might as well pull in," Nancy said. "She knows we're here."

Nancy pulled into the space right next to Teresa's car. Teresa got out of her car and marched over to Nancy's window.

"Just what do you think you're doing?" Teresa demanded angrily. "Why are you following me?"

Nancy got out of the car and faced the woman. "I have reason to suspect that you are behind several threats that have occurred at Steadman's," she said coolly.

"And why would you possibly suspect me?" Teresa asked, her eyebrows raised in a haughty expression.

Nancy reached into her pocket and pulled out the red bandanna. "This is the main reason," she said. "You were wearing it yesterday."

"Where did you get that?" Teresa snapped. She tried to snatch it away, but Nancy tossed it into the car window behind her.

"Next to the swimming pool last night," Nancy said calmly, "where someone nearly drowned me. When I got away and turned on the lights, I found your red bandanna near the spot where I was grabbed."

Teresa's face had become ashen while Nancy explained, and a look of disbelief had come into her eyes.

"That bandanna was stolen from me," Teresa said.

"Oh?" Nancy said. "When?"

"Last evening," Teresa said. "Someone broke into my cottage. The bandanna was the only thing taken."

"Did you report this to Henry Steadman?"

Teresa snorted. "Report a stolen bandanna? Are you kidding?"

"Well, you still haven't told me why you were at the island," Nancy said. "And before you tell me that you weren't there, I'd like to remind you that you are the most likely suspect for an attempted murder charge."

Teresa studied Nancy for a moment. Then she shrugged. "I was fishing," she said. "I like to fish."

Nancy stared at the woman in front of her. She had seemed genuinely shocked by the story of Nancy's near-drowning experience. Or was she simply horrified that she had been caught? Her fishing story was hard to accept.

There was nothing else Nancy could do at the moment. She got back into her car, and the three girls headed back to the resort.

"I don't believe that crazy story about her bandanna being stolen," Bess said.

"It's no crazier a story than anything else going on here," Nancy replied.

"Well, that's true," admitted Bess.

"So what now?" George asked.

"I think the key to everything is at Horse Island," Nancy said. "It's time for a return visit."

Bess looked at Nancy as if she didn't believe what she'd just heard. "Nancy, no!" she cried.

Nancy smiled. "I think you and George should stay back at the resort. Keep your eyes open and see if anyone takes off in a boat after I go."

"I don't like this one bit," Bess insisted. "It's too dangerous."

"I'll be okay," Nancy assured her.

The girls arrived back at Steadman's and had a quick lunch. Nancy didn't prepare for her trip quietly. In fact, she was determined to let everyone know exactly where she was going. She talked openly with guests in the dining room and to several guests around the boat house, making sure they all knew her destination was Horse Island.

She got in her canoe, pushed off from the shore, and waved goodbye to Bess and George. "See you later," she called to them. "Maybe I'll see a few ghosts!"

She hoped to lure the person—or persons—responsible for the snake, the prowling, the ransacking, the hanging dummy, the stolen canoe, the poison berries, the fire, and the near-drowning. She didn't know yet what the connection was between Horse Island and the incidents at the resort. She would figure that out later. So far, the culprit hadn't really hurt anyone. Nancy was gambling that he or she would stay true to that pattern.

Nancy realized her plan had worked when she was halfway across the lake. She turned and saw the pinpoint of a figure in a canoe.

She was being followed.

13

A Trap Is Sprung

When Nancy neared the island, she paddled into the cove that Teresa had used the day before. There she dragged her canoe behind a large rock and then hid herself behind some bushes.

She could see the figure approaching in the lake and squinted to see who it was. She wasn't surprised.

Teresa Diamond paddled her canoe and looked furtively around the shore, apparently trying to find Nancy. While Teresa pulled her canoe up on shore down the beach from the cove, Nancy emerged from behind the bushes and headed inland toward the old house.

Without turning around, Nancy knew that Teresa had spotted her. She could hear Teresa's footsteps behind her. Nancy adjusted the knapsack on her back and kept walking.

The afternoon was warm, and Nancy felt the hot sun on the back of her neck. She wondered if she'd see the horses on the island today. She made a mental note to stay away from the large open areas so that she wouldn't be caught in front of a stampede again.

The house loomed up ahead of her. She wondered what Teresa had in mind. Was she carrying a weapon? Had she followed Nancy to hurt her? To deliver another potentially deadly warning?

Suddenly there was a cry from behind Nancy. She whirled around, expecting to see Teresa. But no one was there.

The cry came again, a cry for help.

"Teresa?" Nancy shouted back. "Teresa?"

"Help me!" came the anguished cry.

Was Teresa in trouble? Or was this a trick?

Nancy took a step toward the cries. "Where are you?" she shouted.

"Here!" came Teresa's answer. "In here!"

Nancy began walking toward the voice, her heart pounding. Logic told her that she was walking into a trap. Yet how could she leave, not knowing whether or not Teresa was hurt?

"Here!" Teresa shouted. "I'm down here!"

"Where?" Nancy called out as she turned in a circle. "Where are you?"

"Down here!" Teresa yelled. "In this pit!"

It was then that Nancy saw where Teresa was hidden. She *was* in a pit, about ten steps away. It was a hole at least eight feet deep that had been dug into the ground. Thick brush surrounded the pit and fell into its depths.

"This is a trap!" Nancy gasped, walking over to the pit.

"I didn't even see it," Teresa said from the bottom of the pit. She stood there, now a small figure, looking up at Nancy. "It was covered with brush. Hey, get me out of here, will you?"

Nancy dropped her knapsack and took a quick look around her. "I need some kind of rope or something I can drop down to you." She searched through the nearby brush and trees for a long vine or large branch she could drag to the pit for Teresa to climb. She found nothing.

"What's taking so long?" Teresa asked anxiously from the bottom of the pit.

"I'm looking for something to throw to you to pull you up—" Nancy stopped, an idea flashing in her head. "I'll be right back."

"Swell. I'll be right here," Teresa said. "I'm not going anywhere."

Nancy dashed up to the old house, around to

the back, and let herself in the back door. She ran into the parlor and grabbed all the sheets off the furniture. She wadded them into a huge ball and raced out of the house, back to where Teresa was caught in the pit.

"I'm going to tie these sheets together," Nancy called to her. "I need to reach this tree over here, so it'll take about four sheets."

Teresa nodded.

Nancy tied the corners of four sheets together and tossed one end down to Teresa. Then she wrapped the other end around the nearest tree, which was thin but sturdy.

"Okay!" she yelled to Teresa. "You can climb up now." She held tightly to her end and pulled with all her strength.

Within half a minute Teresa's head appeared at the edge of the pit, then her shoulders and arms. She threw a leg over the top and climbed up on solid ground.

Nancy released her end of the sheets and joined Teresa at the edge of the pit. Both of them sat on the ground, resting from their exertion.

"Who would do this?" Nancy wondered aloud. "And why?"

"As you said, it's a trap," Teresa replied.

"But who wants to capture humans on Horse Island?" Nancy asked, getting to her feet.

Teresa stood up but didn't speak. She only shrugged and looked away.

Nancy turned to face her. "Teresa," she said, "why did you follow me?"

"I wasn't following you," Teresa said.

"Of course you were," Nancy cried impatiently. "I made a big deal about coming here by myself. It was bait, and you took it." She moved a step closer to Teresa. "*Why?*"

Teresa hesitated for a moment. "I have an interest in the island myself," she said stiffly.

"What kind of interest?" Nancy demanded.

"Professional."

"What does that mean?" Nancy pressed.

"I told you, I'm a writer," Teresa said.

"A novelist?"

Teresa eyed Nancy directly. "It's a project that I can't talk about right now." She turned and took a step away. Then she stopped and turned back to Nancy. "Sorry."

Nancy didn't respond.

"Thanks for the help," Teresa said softly. "I really mean that."

Nancy scanned the area around them. "I wonder if there are other pits around here."

"That's a good point," Teresa said. "There may be. You'd better be careful."

Nancy gazed at Teresa a moment. "Are you aware that there is a new fence on the other side of those trees?" She nodded toward the woods.

Teresa didn't speak for a moment. Then she said, "How do you know it's new?"

"The wood is new," Nancy said. "It hasn't been weathered. Come with me—I'll show you."

"No," said Teresa. "I have—things I have to do now."

Nancy didn't speak but held Teresa's gaze.

Teresa sighed. "I'm an investigative reporter," she said finally. "I'm working on a story here on the island, and I can't say any more about it."

"Okay," Nancy said. "Thank you for telling me that much."

Teresa nodded, turned, and walked back toward the cove. That made Nancy curious. Was she leaving?

Nancy sat down behind a clump of trees and watched Teresa. The woman got into her canoe and pushed out into the water. She looked out over the water and waved her arm. Nancy saw a tiny figure in a motorboat waving back at Teresa.

Nancy kept watching as the figure in the boat got closer. It looked like a man. Just as the boat approached Teresa, Nancy recognized who it was.

Rodney Starr, the guy who took care of the horses! Why would he be out here talking to Teresa? Nancy wondered.

The two spoke for a few minutes, and Rodney's gaze shifted to the island. Then he nodded at Teresa, turned his boat around, and motored back toward Steadman's. Teresa kept paddling toward the resort.

What could those two people have to talk about? Nancy thought. If Teresa really *is* an investigative reporter, what has she discovered on the island that is so interesting? And how does Rodney fit into all of this?

Nancy stood when she was sure neither Rodney nor Teresa could see her from their boats and turned to head toward the old house. Just then the air was shattered by the sound of a gunshot!

14

Shots Are Fired

Instinctively Nancy ducked for cover. After a moment she looked up. The only sounds were the gentle rustle of trees blowing in the breeze and the chirping of birds. Hunters, thought Nancy. Maybe it was time to see exactly who those hunters were.

Keeping low, Nancy made her way deeper into the island. She passed the mansion and continued into the woods. Stepping carefully through the underbrush to avoid any other hidden traps, Nancy kept a sharp eye out for hunters but saw no one.

Nancy also stayed alert for the sound of stampeding horses. She began thinking about the wild animals, their speed, their beauty, their strength. If it hadn't been such a dangerous situation, she would have enjoyed seeing the horses galloping by her, their manes blowing in the wind, their hooves pounding rhythmically as they flew by.

It was a shame that the Steadmans' guests could not enjoy seeing the wild horses—even from a distance. Henry had said that the horses were protected by law, but—

Nancy suddenly had a horrifying thought. Were the *horses* being shot by the hunters on the island? Could the hunters be shooting those beautiful creatures? Nancy shuddered.

Shifting her direction slightly, Nancy decided to check out the new fence she had seen earlier with Bess and George.

Could the fence have anything to do with the horses? The hunters? Why had it been erected so recently? And, as George had asked, was it fencing something *in,* or fencing somebody *out?*

Nancy quickened her pace and moved along through the clearing and into a thin layer of woods.

The underbrush abruptly became thicker there, and Nancy stopped suddenly and gasped. *Another trap!* She had nearly stepped into it!

Her heart beating hard, she picked up some of the brush at her feet. A deep pit lay under it. Some twigs fell into its depths and disappeared.

Nancy kicked aside more of the small branches and leaves hiding the trap and gazed into the pit. It appeared to be about the same size as the trap that Teresa had fallen into. Nancy uncovered the rest of the pit and left it that way so that no one else would get hurt.

Bang! Once again, a gun's explosion cracked the peaceful silence of the island.

This shot was even closer. Nancy's heart began to pound, and she looked quickly in all directions, alert for movement in the brush.

Suddenly she heard the thunderlike sound she had heard the day before. This time she immediately recognized the sound of stampeding horses.

She walked on through the woods until the fence came into view, right where she and the girls had seen it before. But something was different.

The building of the fence had been completed. It was now a makeshift corral, the fence extending around in a large circle. Nancy was amazed to see that penned up inside the corral were almost a dozen beautiful wild horses!

Nancy stared in awe at the animals. They were

skittish and nervous, running back and forth and around the enclosed circle.

She took a few steps closer, and the horses, sensing danger, ran to the far side of the corral, whinnying and snorting anxiously. These horses are certainly wild, Nancy thought. They are obviously not used to being around humans.

Nancy looked around her. Apparently she was alone with the animals. At least Nancy couldn't see anyone. But she had the uncomfortable feeling that she was being watched. And she knew for certain there was at least one other person on the island—the person who had fired that shot.

She fixed her gaze on the dense woods beyond. Did she see a movement in the shadows? Was someone standing there watching her? Would that person, realizing that the warnings did no good, decide to do something more dangerous— more deadly?

Nancy walked along the side of the corral, her eyes on the horses. She counted ten of them, but the corral could hold more. Had someone gone to round up more horses?

And what then? What was to be done with the animals? Would they be tamed and sold? What was the purpose of capturing the wild creatures?

Nancy kept walking, and the feeling that she was being watched returned to her.

"Hello?" Nancy called out.

There was no answer.

"Is anyone there?" She directed her question to the woods, where she thought she had seen movement, but all was still.

Nancy continued her walk along the side of the corral. Something blue caught her eye up ahead. She focused on it. It appeared to be caught on the gate to the corral. Reaching the gate, she found that it was a piece of cotton. Its edges were uneven and rough, as if it had been torn away from a larger piece of cloth. Carefully she freed it from the gate's latch and slipped it into her knapsack.

Nancy continued her walk around the corral. The horses were aware of her every move, and they nervously edged away, snorting as soon as she got close.

Up ahead a footprint caught her eye. She hurried over to it and squatted. Then Nancy saw that there were several of them. The ground was still soft from the heavy rain two days before. The prints were large, mostly made by a man or a large woman, and sunken into the earth about an eighth of an inch. They appeared to be from shoes with a pattern of treads on the soles.

Nancy was so busy inspecting the footprint that she didn't realize someone was approaching from behind. The next thing she knew, a searing pain shot through the back of her head and stunned her.

And then Nancy was enveloped in blackness.

15

Face-to-Face

Nancy tried to look out through the haze in front of her eyes but could see nothing. Her head ached, and she lay on something hard. She attempted to focus her eyes, strained to move her arms and legs. They wouldn't work, and the effort was exhausting. The blackness crept up on her, and she fought it until she had no strength left.

When she opened her eyes again she was able to see more clearly. Her head still ached, but her mind was sharper, although she had no idea how long she had been unconscious. She looked around and realized she was lying on the floor in the parlor of the old house. Her hands and feet were tied together.

"Well, well, well. The intrepid young detective."

Nancy knew who was speaking before she saw him. She looked up to see Steve Matheson sitting in a large overstuffed chair halfway across the room. He was wearing jeans and a red polo shirt, and his sunglasses were perched on his head. "Did you have a nice nap?"

"I suppose I can thank you for the whack on the head," she said defiantly.

"I'm afraid so," he admitted. "I bet you're surprised it's me, huh?"

"Not really," she told him. "I was beginning to suspect you. I know it was you Bess saw standing out in the woods that night when we were stranded on the island."

"What makes you think that?" he asked calmly.

"Those sunglasses," Nancy said.

"You can't prove they were mine."

"No," Nancy said, "but I'm pretty certain they were. They were prescription sunglasses, which I noticed you wear."

"So do a lot of people."

"Yes, but the next day you didn't have your sunglasses on. It was a bright, sunny day. If you hadn't lost your glasses, you would have had them on."

Steve's face turned red.

"And I'll bet," Nancy continued, "that those glasses on your head now are new. You had them made on that trip into town for 'supplies,' didn't you?"

Steve regained his composure. "Okay, so it was me. I was already here on the island when you girls arrived. I set your canoe adrift."

"And you were the ghost staring into the window," added Nancy.

"Whoever locked that kitchen door was pretty smart," said Steve. "I had some plans that were going to scare the three of you out of this house and into the storm." He chuckled ruefully. "But I was the one who got stuck outside. So I made the best of it and pretended to be a ghost."

"You're responsible for all the creepy things that have been going on, aren't you?" said Nancy.

"I had a little help," Steve said, a tight smile creeping across his face.

"Oh?" said Nancy. "Who was that?"

Steve shrugged. "You're so smart, you tell me."

"Okay," Nancy said. "How about Rodney Starr?"

Steve's mouth dropped open. "How'd you—"

"You needed someone who knew about horses, didn't you?" Nancy said.

"Yup. Rodney's my man. He did his share of

the dirty tricks. He set up the dummy and started the fire, though they were both my ideas."

"I'll bet it was you who tried to drown me, though," Nancy accused, instinctively knowing that Steve was the more brutal of the two men.

"If I had wanted to drown you, I *would* have," Steve said angrily. "I was hoping a warning would be enough. But apparently it wasn't."

"You stole Teresa's bandanna to make it look as if *she* was the one who tried to kill me."

"I thought I'd get rid of two problems at once," said Steve.

"What sort of problem was Teresa?" Nancy asked. "Was she investigating you?"

"I don't know what she knew, or who told her," Steve admitted. "But she was snooping around the island, and I didn't like it. I broke into her cabin and found the story she had written for a newspaper. I poured some red ink over every page, hoping to scare her."

"She didn't get scared, though," said Nancy.

"No. It's a shame, too. After I'm done with you, she'll be the next to meet with an accident. Two mysterious accidents in one summer. That should finish off the Steadman Resort."

Nancy tried not to let his words panic her. More than ever before, she needed to stay calm.

"Why are you out to close the resort?" she asked. "It has to do with the horses, doesn't it?"

Steve laughed. "Right again, super sleuth. I discovered that there were wild horses here last summer. There's a fortune in horses here for the taking. The only thing standing between me and the horses is that stupid resort. Once the Steadmans are out of business, there will be no one around for miles who will be able to see what I'm doing."

"And what exactly will you be doing?" asked Nancy coolly.

Steve hesitated for a moment. "Well, I guess you know too much already. You're not going to be around to tell anyone, anyway. I'm going to continue capturing the horses and then sell some of them to breeders. Then, with the money, I plan to buy the resort from Steadman and start a dude ranch of my own."

"He'll never sell his land to you," Nancy said disdainfully.

"He will after I've ruined the reputation of his place. Once the business dies down, he'll be willing to sell the place for next to nothing. I started out hoping no one would get hurt, but I've come too far to turn back now. I've been poor all my life, and I'm sick of it. These horses are going to bring me a fortune, and nothing's going to stop me."

"Why did you dig those pits?" Nancy asked.

"To keep nosy people like you and Teresa away from the center of the island. So you found one of them, huh?"

"Teresa did," Nancy said. "I helped her get out."

"Too bad," Steve said. "Now I'll have to come up with a foolproof plan for taking care of Miss Diamond."

"Those shots we heard," Nancy said. "They weren't hunters, were they?"

Steve laughed. "What a great story that was!" He seemed proud of himself. "It served two purposes: We scared away a lot of people who might've come over to the island to explore, and we used the shots to startle the horses and get them running where we wanted them to go."

"Yes," Nancy said. "It was very clever."

"But now that you know everything," said Steve, "I can't let you go back to the resort and tell everybody." He smiled. "I guess I'm going to have to arrange a little boating accident for you." His grin widened. "Maybe *your* ghost will be haunting this island, too."

"Those ghost stories came in handy for you,

didn't they?" Nancy said, making an effort to stay calm. "You used them to help scare people away."

Steve laughed again. "Those ghost stories have been around for years. People believe what they want to believe." He got up and stretched. "Well, I'm going out to tend to the horses. I'll be back later to set you up for your little accident." He disappeared into the dining room. A few moments later, Nancy heard him go out the kitchen door.

Immediately she set to work trying to loosen her bonds, but the knots were expertly tied and wouldn't budge.

Nancy slumped back against the couch and tried to come up with a plan. The ticking of the old clock was the only sound in the quiet room. That's it! she thought. The clock.

Wriggling to her feet, Nancy hopped to the mantel across the room. She looked up at the clock. It was a shame to damage the antique, but she had to.

"Here goes," she muttered as she pushed the clock off the mantel with her tied hands. *Smash!* The glass face of the clock shattered on the floor.

Nancy stooped and picked up the largest shard of glass. Its edge was razor sharp. Clasping it in her fingers, she began sawing at the ropes around her feet. In five minutes her feet were free.

Cutting the ropes binding her hands was more difficult. It was hard to get the glass at the right angle. She had just finished when a noise at the back door made her look up.

Steve Matheson was returning!

With the front door boarded over, the only way out was the back door. But that escape route was impossible now.

Nancy hurried to the front foyer and up the wide staircase to the second floor. When she got to the top of the stairs, she heard Steve walk into the parlor and cry out when he discovered that she was gone.

Nancy heard him as he began searching the main floor.

It was only a matter of time, Nancy realized, until he would come upstairs to look for her. She had to find a hiding place.

Quietly she crept into the first room at the top of the stairs, the room with the steps leading to the tower.

She looked at the door leading to the tower stairs. The old iron key was still in the lock. That gave her an idea. It was a risky, desperate plan, but it might work.

"Here goes," she said to herself as she slammed the bedroom door that led to the hallway. That was sure to alert Steve. She listened. Almost immediately she heard his steps running up the stairs.

Next she slipped the iron key into her pocket and hurried up the stairs to the shadowy tower. A quick fluttering of bat wings from the room above made her shudder, but she kept climbing the stairs. It was day, the time when the nocturnal creatures would be sleeping. Nancy moved as quietly as she could. Her plan depended on not disturbing the sleeping bats.

At the top of the stairs was a round, dimly lit room. Dusty boxes and trunks were the only furniture. Looking up, Nancy saw that the rafters of the old room were crowded with bats. "Perfect," she whispered, fighting down a quiver of revulsion.

Come and get me, Steve, thought Nancy, crouching behind a large, upright trunk near the stairs. "Come on up," Nancy whispered as she kept a close watch on the bats above.

The door to the tower opened. Nancy held her breath and hoped Steve didn't discover the bats too soon.

Nancy heard his steps coming closer, but she

didn't dare peek out from her hiding place. She had to wait until he was in the tower. Her gaze fell on an old pincushion sitting in the dust at her feet. She picked it up. It was just what she needed.

Steve was now at the top of the stairs. Nancy could see his head over the old trunk.

He walked into the room, looking for her. He saw a pile of boxes on the far side of the room next to a window and moved toward them. "I know you're—"

But before he finished the sentence, Nancy hurled the pincushion at a group of bats roosting in the rafters. They immediately dropped into the air and began swooping around the tower room. Steve cried out and covered his head with his hands.

Nancy was ready for this chance to escape, and she jumped up, running out from behind the trunk and straight down the stairs as fast as she could.

"Nancy!" he cried out. Still covering his head, he started after her.

Nancy reached the bottom of the stairs, slammed the door, and locked it. Steve reached the other side of the door almost instantly.

"Open this door!" he hollered, banging with

his fist and kicking. Nancy looked at the rattling doorknob with alarm. It was very old. Would the lock hold?

Nancy didn't intend to wait and find out. She flew out of the empty bedroom and took the front stairs two at a time, her heart beating frantically all the way. At the bottom of the staircase, she ran through the foyer, toward the back door. But the sound of a creaking door opening into the kitchen caused her to skid to try to stop from entering the room.

Who could it possibly be? Nancy wondered, just as Teresa, Rodney, the sheriff, and a deputy walked into the room.

16

Now . . . for the Vacation

"Well," said Bess, raising her glass to Nancy, "I'm glad the scary stuff is over so we can relax for a couple of days! I think I'll spend all day tomorrow lying in the sun at the swimming pool."

"You girls deserve it!" said Henry Steadman. "In fact, I'm going to treat you three to an extra week." Nancy, Bess, and George beamed. "I am indebted to you girls for the excellent work you did tracking down the source of all our troubles. Especially you, Nancy."

Nancy grinned and looked around the large round table in the corner of the dining room. Henry sat in the corner spot with his arm around Ruth. Nancy thought the couple looked happier and more relaxed than they had at any time since she and the girls had arrived at the resort. Teresa, Bess, and George sat in the other chairs at the table. For the first time, Teresa was smiling broadly and chatting with the girls. She, too, appeared to be relieved that the tension of the past several days was over.

"There's one thing I still don't understand," Bess said to Teresa. "How did you know about the plans Steve had for the horses on the island?"

"I had an anonymous tip," Teresa said. "I figured out a few days after I arrived here that it was Rodney Starr who had called me at the paper. Rodney kept avoiding me, and I saw him talking with Steve several times. Rodney had gotten involved with Steve because he needed the money. But when he saw those beautiful horses and realized that he was going to play a part in capturing them, he couldn't go through with it."

"Why didn't he just tell Steve he'd changed his mind?" Bess asked.

"Well," Teresa said, "I think Rodney realized that Steve could become dangerous. I think he was afraid of what Steve might do. So he contacted me and pretended to play along with Steve."

147

"So Rodney *did* set the dummy in the trees," George said.

"Yes. That was harmless enough, although it scared off some of the guests," Teresa said. "He finally admitted to me that he was the person who had tipped me off. But he wouldn't tell me exactly what was happening. He just led me along, telling me to visit the island with my camera at certain times. He wanted me to 'discover' what was going on while he pretended to play along."

"Will Rodney go to jail?" Bess asked.

Nancy shook her head. "The sheriff said that because of his cooperation with the police, he probably won't be charged. But you can bet Steve is going away for a long time."

"Good," Henry said.

"Speaking of the sheriff," Nancy said, "which one of you decided I needed help and called him?"

Bess and George both said, "We did." Then George went on. "We were on shore waiting for you to come back from the island when we heard the gunshots. We called the sheriff, and when he and his deputy arrived, Teresa and Rodney showed up and told them what was going on."

"Teresa," Nancy asked, "was that call you

made at the phone booth to your newspaper editor?"

"Yes," Teresa said. She smiled. "When you're an investigative reporter you have to keep everything a secret. I thought you might be a reporter for a rival newspaper trying to get the scoop before I did. That's why I called from the phone booth in town instead of using the phone in my cottage."

"Well," Henry said, laughing, "I can't tell you how relieved I am that Otis wasn't involved in all this. Steve confessed to putting the poison berries in the dessert. Otis had nothing to do with it."

"Yes," Ruth said, "I'm relieved, too. He's a tyrant, but I was wrong to think the worst of him. He just believes he's the world's best cook and thinks his pay should reflect that."

"Well," Bess said, taking a bite of her broiled lake trout, "I would have to agree with him on that point. He *is* the world's best! The food here is better than any I've ever tasted!"

"I think maybe it's time to renegotiate his salary," Henry said to Ruth.

"I think you're right," Ruth agreed. "He *is* a brilliant chef."

Just then the Burkle sisters walked up to the piano, and the spotlight hit them.

"Hi, everybody!" Carrie said, tossing back her

red curls."I'm Carrie, and this is my older sister, Ann."

"Just a year older," Ann reminded her.

"Well, fifteen months," Carrie said.

"Okay, okay," Ann said, and she let out a sigh. The diners chuckled.

"We're going to entertain you tonight," Carrie said. Her gaze swept over the audience and stopped at Nancy. "Oh, hey, there's Nancy Drew!" she cried. "Pete, put the spot on Nancy, will you?"

Suddenly Nancy was in the spotlight.

"You see this person?" Carrie said. "She's a terrific detective. She saved the Steadman Resort from a mean guy who wanted to bring this great place down. Let's all give her a big hand!"

The diners applauded, and Nancy's face grew pink.

"Now we're going to do one of our favorite songs," Carrie said. She introduced their pianist and their first number.

"Oh, by the way," Teresa said, leaning over toward Nancy, "when I do the piece about the capturing of the wild horses at Horse Island, you'll be a big part of the story."

"Me?" Nancy said.

"Sure," said Teresa. "You were incredible. What I worked on for a whole week, you came along and wrapped up in just a few days! You deserve the credit."

"She is the best, isn't she?" said Bess proudly.

"That's our Nancy," agreed George.

Henry lifted his glass and grinned. "I thank you, my wife thanks you, and the wild horses of Horse Island thank you," he teased.

"My pleasure," Nancy replied, smiling. "Steve Matheson should have known his plan didn't stand a ghost of a chance."

"Please!" cried Bess, covering her ears. "I never want to hear the word *ghost* again!" Everyone laughed while the Burkle sisters sang on into the summer night.

THE HARDY BOYS® SERIES By Franklin W. Dixon

☐	#59: NIGHT OF THE WEREWOLF	70993-3/$3.50	☐	#92: THE SHADOW KILLERS	66309-7/$3.99
☐	#60: MYSTERY OF THE SAMURAI		☐	#93: THE SEPENT'S TOOTH	
	SWORD	67302-5/$3.99		MYSTERY	66310-0/$3.50
☐	#61: THE PENTAGON SPY	67221-5/$3.99		#94: BREAKDOWN IN AXEBLADE	66311-9/$3.50
☐	#62: THE APEMAN'S SECRET	69068-X/$3.50	☐	#95: DANGER ON THE AIR	66305-4/$3.50
☐	#63: THE MUMMY CASE	64289-8/$3.99	☐	#96: WIPEOUT	66306-2/$3.50
☐	#64: MYSTERY OF SMUGGLERS COVE	66229-5/$3.50	☐	#97: CAST OF CRIMINALS	66307-0/$3.50
☐	#65: THE STONE IDOL	69402-2/$3.50	☐	#98: SPARK OF SUSPICION	66304-6/$3.99
☐	#66: THE VANISHING THIEVES	63890-4/$3.99	☐	#99: DUNGEON OF DOOM	69449-9/$3.50
☐	#67: THE OUTLAW"S SILVER	74229-9/$3.50	☐	#100: THE SECRET OF ISLAND	
☐	#68: DEADLY CHASE	62477-6/$3.50		TREASURE	69450-2/$3.50
☐	#69: THE FOUR-HEADED DRAGON	65797-6/$3.50		#101: THE MONEY HUNT	69451-0/$3.50
☐	#70: THE INFINITY CLUE	69154-6/$3.50		#102: TERMINAL SHOCK	69288-7/$3.50
☐	#71: TRACK OF THE ZOMBIE	62623-X/$3.50		#103: THE MILLION-DOLLAR	
☐	#72: THE VOODOO PLOT	64287-1/$3.99		NIGHTMARE	69272-0/$3.99
☐	#73: THE BILLION DOLLAR			#104: TRICKS OF THE TRADE	69273-9/$3.50
	RANSOM	66228-7/$3.50	☐	#105: THE SMOKE SCREEN	
☐	#74: TIC-TAC TERROR	66858-7/$3.50		MYSTERY	69274-7/$3.99
☐	#75: TRAPPED AT SEA	64290-1/$3.50		#106: ATTACK OF THE	
☐	#76: GAME PLAN FOR DISASTER	72321-9/$3.50	☐	VIDEO VILLIANS	69275-5/$3.99
☐	#77: THE CRIMSON FLAME	64286-3/$3.99		#107: PANIC ON GULL ISLAND	69276-3/$3.99
☐	#78: CAVE IN	69486-3/$3.50	☐	#108: FEAR ON WHEELS	69277-1/$3.99
☐	#79: SKY SABOTAGE	62625-6/$3.50	☐	#109: THE PRIME-TIME CRIME	69278-X/$3.50
☐	#80: THE ROARING RIVER		☐	#110: THE SECRET OF SIGMA SEVEN	72717-6/$3.99
	MYSTERY	73004-5/$3.50	☐	#111: THREE-RING TERROR	73057-6/$3.99
☐	#81: THE DEMON'S DEN	62622-1/$3.50	☐	#112: THE DEMOLITION MISSION	73058-4/$3.99
☐	#82: THE BLACKWING PUZZLE	70472-9/$3.50	☐	#113: RADICAL MOVES	73060-6/$3.99
☐	#83: THE SWAMP MONSTER	49727-8/$3.50	☐	#114: THE CASE OF THE	
☐	#84: REVENGE OF THE DESERT		☐	COUNTERFEIT CRIMINALS	73061-4/$3.99
	PHANTOM	49729-4/$3.50		#115: SABOTAGE AT SPORTS CITY	73062-2/$3.99
☐	#85: SKYFIRE PUZZLE	67458-7/$3.50	☐	#116: ROCK 'N' ROLL RENEGADES	73063-0/$3.99
☐	#86: THE MYSTERY OF THE		☐	#117: THE BASEBALL CARD CONSPIRACY	73064-9/$3.99
	SILVER STAR	64374-6/$3.50	☐	#118: DANGER IN THE FOURTH DIMENSION	79308-X/$3.99
☐	#87: PROGRAM FOR DESTRUCTION	64895-0/$3.99	☐	#119: TROUBLE AT COYOTE CANYON	79309-8/$3.99
☐	#88: TRICKY BUSINESS	64973-6/$3.99	☐	#120: CASE OF THE COSMIC KIDNAPPING	79310-1/$3.99
☐	#89: THE SKY BLUE FRAME	64974-4/$3.50	☐	#121: MYSTERY IN THE OLD MINE	79311-X/$3.99
☐	#90: DANGER ON THE DIAMOND	63425-9/$3.99	☐	#122: CARNIVAL OF CRIME	79312-8/$3.99
☐	#91: SHIELD OF FEAR	66308-9/$3.50	☐	#123: ROBOT'S REVENGE	79313-6/$3.99